AN EXCEPTION
TO HIS RULE

AN EXCEPTION TO HIS RULE

BY

LINDSAY ARMSTRONG

MILLS
BOON®

First published in Great Britain 2014
by Mills & Boon, an imprint of Harlequin (UK) Limited,
Large Print edition 2014
Eton House, 18-24 Paradise Road,
Richmond, Surrey, TW9 1SR

© 2014 Lindsay Armstrong

ISBN: 978 0 263 24073 3

Harlequin (UK) Limited's policy is to use papers that
are natural, renewable and recyclable products and made
from wood grown in sustainable forests. The logging
and manufacturing processes conform to the legal
environmental regulations of the country of origin.

Printed and bound in Great Britain
by CPI Antony Rowe, Chippenham, Wiltshire

For my family, Dave, Susie, Matt, Sally, Anabel and David for all their patience.

And my editor, Megan Haslam, for all *her* patience!

For my sister, Carol, whom Mum and I
loved unconditionally all of their lives.

Always in our hearts and in our
thoughts. xx

CHAPTER ONE

DAMIEN WYATT WAS lounging in an upstairs study.

He wore jeans, a khaki bush shirt and desert boots, all visible since his feet were up on the desk. His dark hair was ruffled and there were blue shadows on his jaw.

The windows were open and the roses in the garden below were in bloom. So was the star jasmine creeper clinging to the house. Beyond the garden wall a beach curved around a blue, inviting bay. You could hear the sound of the waves on the beach and there was a tang of salt in the air.

'Hang on,' he said with a sudden frown. 'Is it remotely possible that this Ms *Livingstone* we're talking about is actually *Harriet* Livingstone? Because, if so, forget it, Arthur.'

Arthur Tindall, art connoisseur and colourful dresser—he wore jeans and a yellow waistcoat patterned with black elephants over a maroon shirt—looked confused. 'You've met her?' he asked from the other side of the desk.

'I don't know. Unless there are two Harriet Livingstones, I may have,' Damien said dryly.

'There could well be. Two, I mean,' Arthur replied. 'After all, it's not the wilds of Africa where it was highly unlikely there'd be more than one *Doctor* Livingstone popping up out of nowhere.'

Damien grinned fleetingly. 'I take your point.' He sobered. 'What's your Harriet like? Tall, thin girl with wild hair and an unusual taste in clothing?' He raised an enquiring eyebrow.

Arthur looked blank for a moment. 'Tall, yes,' he said slowly. 'Otherwise, well, certainly not fat and her clothes are—I don't seem to remember much about her clothes.'

'Have you actually met her?' Damien enquired with some irony.

'Of course.' Arthur looked offended then brightened. 'I can tell you one thing: she has very long legs!'

'So does a stork,' Damien observed. 'I couldn't tell with my Ms Livingstone,' he added. 'I mean for someone that tall she obviously had long legs but whether they were—shapely—I couldn't say because they were all covered up in some kind of wraparound batik skirt.'

Arthur stared narrowly into the distance as if trying to conjure up a batik wraparound skirt then he blinked again and said triumphantly, 'Glasses! Large, round, red-rimmed glasses. Also...' he frowned and concentrated '...a rather vague air, although that may be due to being short-sighted, but as if her mind is on higher things.' He grimaced.

Damien Wyatt smiled unpleasantly. 'If it is the same girl, she ran into me about two months ago.

At the same time she was wearing large, round, red-rimmed glasses,' he added significantly.

'Oh, dear! Not the Aston? Oh, *dear*,' Arthur repeated.

Damien looked at him ironically. 'That's putting it mildly. She had no insurance other than compulsory third party and the...*tank* she was driving survived virtually unscathed.'

'Tank?'

Damien shrugged. 'It might as well have been: a solid old four-wheel drive with bull bars.'

This time Arthur winced visibly. 'How did it happen?'

'She swerved to avoid a dog then froze and couldn't correct things until it was too late.' Damien Wyatt drummed his fingers on his desk.

'Was anyone hurt?'

Damien looked at him, his expression sardonic. 'The dog was retrieved by its owner *completely* unscathed. All she broke were her glasses.'

He paused as he recalled the melee after the accident and the curious fact—curious from the point of view that it should have stuck in his mind—that Harriet Livingstone had possessed a pair of rather stunning blue eyes.

'That's not *too* bad,' Arthur murmured.

'That's not all,' Damien remarked acidly. 'I broke my collarbone and the damage to my car was, well—' he shrugged '—the whole exercise cost me a small fortune.'

Arthur forbore to make the obvious comment that a small fortune would hardly make the slightest dent in the very large fortune Damien Wyatt owned.

But Damien continued with palpable sarcasm, 'Therefore, dear Arthur, if there's any possibility it's one and the same girl, you do see there's no way I could let her loose here.' He removed his feet from the desk and sat up.

Arthur Tindall discovered he could certainly see something cool, determined and even quite grim in Damien's dark eyes but he also found he wasn't prepared to give up without a fight.

Whether it was the same girl or not, it did

sound like it, he had to admit, but the thing was he'd promised Penny, his young and delicious yet surprisingly manipulative wife, that he would get the Wyatt job for her friend Harriet Livingstone.

He sat forward. 'Damien, even if she's the same girl—although we don't absolutely know that!—she's good,' he said intently. 'She's damn good. So's her provenance. Your mother's collection couldn't be in better hands, believe me! She's worked in one of the most prestigious art auction houses in the country.' Arthur emphasised this with rolling eyes and a wave of his hand. 'Her father was a noted conservator and restorer of paintings and her references are impeccable.'

'All the same, you've just told me she's vague and distracted,' Damien said impatiently. 'And *I've* had the woman literally run into me!'

Arthur said intensely, 'She may be vague over other things but not about her work. I've found her knowledgeable on not only paintings but por-

celain, ceramics, carpets, miniatures—all sorts
of things. And she's experienced in cataloguing.'

'She sounds like a one woman antiques road-
show,' Damien observed caustically.

'No, but she's the one person I could recom-
mend who would have some familiarity with
most of the odds and ends your mother collected. She's the one person who would have
some idea of their value or who to get a valuation
from, some idea of whether they need restoring,
whether they *could* be restored, who could do it
if it was possible, who—'

Damien held up his hand. 'Arthur, I get your
point. But—'

'Of course,' Arthur interrupted, sitting back
and looking magisterial, 'if it is the same girl,
there's the distinct possibility nothing on earth
would induce her to work for you.'

'Why the hell not?'

Arthur shrugged and folded his arms over his
black and yellow waistcoat. 'I have no doubt you

would have been quite scathing towards her at the time of the accident.'

Damien rubbed his jaw. 'I did ask her,' he said reminiscently, 'whether she'd got her driver's licence out of a cornflakes packet.'

Arthur whistled but said, 'I've heard worse. Was that all?'

Damien shrugged. 'I may have said a few other…less than complimentary things. In the heat of the moment, of course. My car *was* smashed. So was my collarbone.'

'Women don't necessarily see things like that in the same way. About cars, I mean.' Arthur waved his hands again. 'Pure excellence, pure *fineness* in a motor vehicle and then to see it all smashed up may not affect them as deeply as a man.'

Damien chewed his lip then shrugged and picked up his phone as it buzzed discreetly.

Arthur got up and wandered over to the windows. It was a lovely view, he mused, but then Heathcote, home to the Wyatt dynasty, was a magnificent property. They ran cattle and grew macadamias with equal success in the Northern Rivers district of New South Wales but it was machinery—farm machinery, and lately mining machinery—that was the backbone of their fortune.

Damien's grandfather had started it all with a tractor he'd designed and manufactured but, so it was said, Damien had tripled it by investing in mining machinery. And all sorts of mining was happening all over Australia, Arthur thought rather ruefully.

His own connection with the Wyatts had started with Damien's father and his interest in art. Together they'd built up a collection to be proud of. Then, seven years ago, both his parents had been lost at sea when their yacht had capsized. Consequently Damien had inherited the collection.

It was the upheaval after this that had brought to light the full extent of his *mother's* collection of objets d'art—something the rest of the family had tended to overlook. In fact it wouldn't be unfair to say that Heathcote was stuffed to the rafters with them. But it had taken several more years for this decision to do something about them to be made, and hence to his advice being sought.

His first inclination had been to suggest that it should all be crated up and sent to an appropriate firm for assessing. Damien, however, supported by his aunt, had been disinclined to allow any of his mother's treasures to leave Heathcote and it had been their suggestion that he look for someone to do the job in situ.

No easy task since Lennox Head, Heathcote's nearest town, was a long way from Sydney and a fair way from Brisbane or the Gold Coast, the nearest large cities.

Therefore, when Penny had presented him with Harriet Livingstone he'd more or less looked upon it as a godsend…

Arthur turned from the view and studied Damien Wyatt, who'd swung his chair so he was partially facing the other way and was still talking on the phone. At thirty-one, Damien was loose-limbed, lean and deceptively powerful. He was well over six feet tall, broad-shouldered and he had the facility to look at ease in any milieu. Yet there was something about him that let you know that whilst he'd be good outdoors, good at battling the elements, good at managing vast properties, good with mechanical things, he'd also be good with women.

He certainly possessed a pair of fine dark eyes that often had a glint in them indicative of a mercurial personality and a lively intelligence.

Not to put too fine a point on it, Arthur ruminated, as his wife Penny had once remarked: you couldn't call Damien exactly handsome but he was devastatingly attractive and masculine.

He also had thick dark hair and he did possess a powerful intellect. Not only that, but he had an affection for getting his own way and a *cutting,* irritable way it was with him at times, as Harriet Livingstone had apparently encountered, poor girl.

So why, Arthur wondered suddenly, if she was the same girl—and he was pretty sure she was—had she been happy for him to go ahead and sound Damien Wyatt out on this job? She must have recognised the name. She must have some very unpleasant memories of the incident.

She must, above all, find it extremely hard to believe he would ever offer her a job after smashing his beloved Aston Martin with a vehicle not unlike a tank and breaking his collarbone.

So what was behind it, this willingness even to meet Damien Wyatt again? Did she have designs on him? Did she, he swallowed at the mere thought, plan to, if she got the job, fleece him of some of his mother's treasures?

'Hello!'

Arthur came back to the present with a start to see that Damien had finished his call and was looking at him enquiringly.

'Sorry,' he said hastily, and sat down again. 'How's Penny?'

Arthur hesitated. Despite the fact that Damien was always unfailingly polite to Penny, it was hard to escape the feeling that he didn't really approve of her.

Or, if not that, Arthur mused further, did Damien view his belated tumble into matrimony after years of bachelorhood with some cynicism? He was now approaching fifty and was twenty years older than Penny.

Probably, he conceded to himself. Not that Damien Wyatt had anything to be superior about on that score. He might not have been twenty years older than his wife but he did have a failed marriage behind him—a very failed marriage.

'Arthur, what's on your mind?'

Once again Arthur came back to the present with a start. 'Nothing!' he asserted.

'You seem to be miles away,' Damien commented. 'Is Penny all right or not?'

'She's fine. She's fine,' Arthur repeated, and

came to another sudden decision, although with an inward grimace. 'Look, Damien, I've changed my mind about Harriet Livingstone. I don't think she's the right one after all. So give me a few days and I'll find someone else.'

It was a penetratingly narrowed dark gaze Damien bestowed on Arthur Tindall. 'That's a rather sudden change of heart,' he drawled.

'Yes, well, a blind man could see you two are unlikely to get along so…' Arthur left his sentence up in the air.

Damien settled more comfortably in his chair. 'Where are you going to find a paragon to equal Ms Livingstone? Or was that a slight exaggeration on your part?' he asked casually enough, although with a load of implied satire.

'No it was not!' Arthur denied. 'And I have no idea where I'm going to find one—be that as it may, I will.'

Damien Wyatt rubbed his jaw. 'I'll have a look at her.'

Arthur sat up indignantly. 'Now look here; you can't change your mind just like that!'

'Not many minutes ago you were hoping to goad me into doing *just* that.'

'*When*?'

'When you told me I'd be the last person on earth she'd work for. You were hoping that would annoy me or simply arouse my contrary streak to the extent I'd change my mind.' Damien's lips twisted. 'Well, I have.'

'Which streak prompted that, do you think? A rather large ego?' Arthur enquired heavily after a moment's thought.

Damien grinned. 'No idea. Bring her here for an interview tomorrow afternoon.'

'Damien—' Arthur rose '—I have to say I can't guarantee the girl.'

'You mean everything you told me about her provenance et cetera—' Damien raised his eyebrows sardonically '—was a lot of bull dust?'

'No,' Arthur denied. 'I followed up every reference she gave me and they all checked out, I've talked to her and sounded her out on a range of art work, as I mentioned, but—'

'Just bring her, Arthur,' Damien interrupted wearily. 'Just bring her.'

Despite this repeated command, Damien Wyatt stayed where he was for a few minutes after Arthur had gone, as he asked himself why he'd done what he'd just done.

No sensible answer presented itself other than that he *had* somehow felt goaded into it, although not because of anything Arthur had said.

So—curiosity, perhaps? Why would Harriet Livingstone want to have anything to do with him after, he had to admit, he'd been pretty unpleasant to her? Some quirky form of revenge?

More likely a quirky form of attaching herself to him, he thought cynically. All the more reason to have stuck to his guns and refused to see the girl.

What else could have been at work behind the

scenes of his mental processes then? he asked himself rather dryly. Boredom?

Surely not. He had enough on his plate at the moment to keep six men busy. He had an overseas trip coming up in a couple of days, and yet…

He stared into the distance with a frown. Of course the possibility remained that it *wasn't* the same girl…

At three o'clock the next afternoon, Harriet Livingstone and Arthur Tindall were shown into the lounge at Heathcote by a tall angular woman with iron-grey hair cut in a short cap. Arthur addressed the woman as Isabel and kissed her on the cheek but didn't introduce her. Arthur was looking worried and distracted.

Damien Wyatt came in from outside through another door, accompanied by a large dog.

He threw his sunglasses onto a side table and said something to the dog, a young, highly bred and powerful Scottish wolfhound, that sat down obligingly although looking keenly alert.

'Ah,' Damien Wyatt said to Arthur after a brief but comprehensive study of Harriet, 'same girl.' He turned back to Harriet. 'We meet again, Miss Livingstone. I'd almost convinced myself you wouldn't be the same person or, if you were, that you wouldn't come.'

Harriet cleared her throat. 'Good afternoon, Mr Wyatt,' she said almost inaudibly.

Damien narrowed his eyes and cast Arthur an interrogative glance but Arthur only looked blank.

Damien returned his attention to Harriet Livingstone.

No batik wraparound skirt today, he noted: an unexceptional navy linen dress instead. Not too long, not too short, not too tight, although it did make her blue eyes even bluer. In fact her outfit was very discreetly elegant and so were her shoes, polished navy leather with little heels. This caused a faint fleeting smile to twist his lips as it crossed his mind that this girl probably rarely, if ever, wore higher heels. And he wondered what it must be like for a girl to be as tall, if not taller, than many of the men she met. Not that she was taller than he was…

Then there was her hair. Shoulder-length, fair and with a tendency to curl, it no longer looked as if she'd been pulled through a bush backwards. It was neatly tied up instead with a black ribbon. Her make-up was minimal. In fact it was all so…what? he asked himself. Well-bred, classic, timeless, discreet—he had no difficulty imagining her in the hallowed halls of some revered antique and art auction company or a museum.

But, and this caused him to frown rather than smile, the main difference between this Harriet Livingstone and the girl who'd run into him was that she was no longer thin. Very slender, perhaps, but no, not exactly skinny.

Despite being slender rather than skinny and despite her more composed outward presentation, it was, however, plain to see that she was strung as taut as a piano wire.

It was also plain to see—and his eyes widened slightly as his gaze travelled down her figure—that her legs were little short of sensational…

'Well,' he said, 'you were right, Arthur, but let's get down to brass tacks. We've organised a few of my mother's things in the dining room. Please come through and give me your opinion of them, Ms Livingstone.'

He moved forward and the dog rose and came with him but stopped to look at Harriet with almost human curiosity. And, as Harriet returned the dog's gaze, just a little of her tension seemed to leave her.

Damien noticed this with a slight narrowing of his eyes. And he said, somewhat to his surprise, 'I'm sorry, I forgot to introduce you—this is Tottie, Miss Livingstone. Her proper name is much more complicated. Something tells me you like dogs?'

Harriet put out a hand for Tottie to inspect.

'Yes. It's one of the reasons I ran into you,' she murmured. 'I thought I'd killed the dog and I—just froze.'

Arthur tut-tutted.

Damien Wyatt blinked, twice. 'Much worse in your estimation than killing me, I gather?'

Harriet Livingstone allowed Tottie to lick her hand then said quietly, 'Of course not. I didn't—I'm sorry but I didn't have time to think about you or anything else. It all happened so fast.'

'I'm suitably damned,' he replied. 'All right, let's get this show on the road.'

'If you're having second thoughts I'd quite understand,' Harriet said politely, with a less than polite glint in her eye, however.

She really doesn't like him, Arthur thought and rubbed his face distractedly. So why is she doing this?

But what Damien said took him even further by surprise. 'On the contrary, after what Arthur has told me about you I'm positively agog to see you in action. Shall I lead on?'

He didn't wait for her response but strode out with Tottie following regally.

Harriet put the exquisite little jade peach tree down on the table with a sigh of pleasure. And her gaze swept over the rest of the treasures spread out on the dining room table. 'They're all lovely—she had marvellous taste, your mother. And judgement.' She took off her red-rimmed glasses.

Damien was leaning his broad shoulders against the mantelpiece with his arms crossed. He did not respond to her admiration of his mother's collection but said, 'Is that a new pair or did you get them fixed?' He nodded towards her glasses resting on the table.

Harriet looked confused for a moment, then, 'Oh, it was only a lens that got broken so I was able to get a new one.'

'Red glasses.' He looked her up and down. 'Not quite in keeping with the restrained elegance of the rest of you—today, that is.'

A fleeting smile twisted Harriet's lips. 'Ah, but it makes them a lot easier to find.' And, for a moment, she thought he was going to smile too but he continued to look unamused.

Harriet looked away.

'How would you catalogue them?' he asked after a moment. 'This is not even one tenth of them, by the way.'

'I'd photograph them in the sequence I came upon them and I'd write an initial summary of them. Then, when they were all itemised—' Harriet laced her fingers '—I'd probably sort them into categories, mainly to make it easier to locate them and I'd write a much more comprehensive description of them, their condition, any research I'd done on them, any work required on them et cetera. I'd also, if your mother kept any receipts or paperwork on them, try to marry it all up.'

'How long do you think that would take?'

Harriet shrugged. 'Hard to say without seeing the full extent of the collection.'

'Months,' Arthur supplied with gloomy conviction.

'Were you aware it was a live-in position, Miss Livingstone?' Damien queried. 'Because we're out in the country here, whoever does the job will spend an awful lot of time travelling otherwise.'

'Yes, Arthur did explain that. I believe there's an old stable block that's been converted to a studio and it has a flat above it. But—' Harriet paused '—weekends would be free, wouldn't they?'

Damien raised an eyebrow. 'Didn't Arthur tell you that?'

'He did,' Harriet agreed, 'but I needed to double-check.'

'A boyfriend you're eager to get back to?' Damien didn't wait for her response. 'If that's going to be a problem and you're forever wanting time off to be with him—'

'Not at all,' Harriet cut across him quite decisively.

'Not at all, you wouldn't be wanting time off all the time or not at all, there is no boyfriend?' Damien enquired.

Arthur coughed. 'Damien, I don't think—' he began but Harriet interrupted him this time.

'It's quite all right, Arthur.' She turned back to Damien. 'Allow me to set your mind at rest, Mr Wyatt. There is no fiancé, no husband, no lovers, in short, no one in my life to distract me in that direction.'

'Well, well,' Damien drawled, 'not only a paragon in your profession but also your private life.'

Harriet Livingstone merely allowed her deep blue gaze to rest on him thoughtfully for a moment or two before she turned away with the tiniest shrug, as if to say he was some kind of rare organism she didn't understand.

Bloody hell, Damien Wyatt found himself thinking as he straightened abruptly, who does she think she is? Not content with smashing my car and causing me considerable discomfort for weeks, she's—

He didn't get to finish this set of thoughts as the woman called Isabel popped her head around the door and offered them afternoon tea.

Arthur looked at his watch. 'Thank you so much, Isabel, but I'm afraid I won't have time. Penny wants me home by four.' He paused. 'What about you, Harriet? We did come in separate cars,' he explained to Damien.

Harriet hesitated and glanced at Damien. And because most of his mental sensors seemed to be honed in on this tall, slender girl, he saw the tension creep back as she picked up her purse and her knuckles whitened.

And he heard himself say something he hadn't expected to say. 'If you'd like a cup of tea, stay by all means, Miss Livingstone. We haven't finished the interview anyway.'

She hesitated again then thanked him quietly.

Isabel retreated and Arthur, looking visibly harassed, subjected them to an involved explanation of why he needed to be home. Plus he was obviously reluctant to miss any of the verbal duel he was witnessing. But he finally left. And the tea tray arrived but this time Damien introduced the bearer as his aunt Isabel, and invited her to join them.

'Sorry,' Isabel said as she put the tea tray down on the coffee table set in front of the settee in a corner of the dining room, 'but I'm popping into Lennox to pick up our dry-cleaning. Please excuse me, Miss Livingstone,' she added.

Harriet nodded somewhat dazedly and once again the door closed, this time on his aunt.

'I don't think there's anyone else who could interrupt us,' Damien Wyatt said with some irony. 'Do sit down and pour the tea.'

Harriet sank down onto the settee and her hand hovered over the tea tray. 'Uh—there's only one cup.'

'I never drink the stuff,' he said dismissively, 'so pour yours and let's get *on* with things.'

Harriet lifted the heavy silver teapot and spilt some tea on the pristine white tray cloth.

Damien swore beneath his breath, and came

over to sit down beside her. 'Put it down and tell me something, Harriet Livingstone—why are you doing this? No, wait.'

He picked up the pot Harriet had relinquished and poured a cup of tea without spilling a drop. Then he indicated the milk and sugar but she shook her head. 'Th-that's fine, just as it comes, thank you.'

He moved the cup and saucer in front of her and offered her a biscuit that looked like home-made shortbread.

She shook her head.

'I can guarantee them. The cook makes them himself,' he said.

'Thank you but no. I—I don't have a sweet tooth.'

He pushed the porcelain biscuit barrel away. 'You look—you don't look as sk—as thin as you did that day,' he amended.

A flicker of amusement touched her mouth. 'Skinny you were going to say? I guess I did. I lost a bit of weight for a time. I've probably always been thin, though.'

'Sorry,' he murmured. 'But look, why *are* you doing this?'

Harriet hesitated and watched the steam rising gently from her tea.

'You obviously haven't forgiven me for the things I said that day,' he continued. 'Most of the time since you've been here you've been a nervous wreck or, if not that, beaming pure hostility my way. The only thing that seems to relax you is contact with my dog or my mother's odds and ends.'

He broke off and looked rueful as Tottie rose, came over and arranged herself at Harriet's feet.

Harriet glanced at him briefly. In jeans, boots and a khaki bush shirt, with his thick hair ruffled and blue shadows on his jaw, he looked the epitome of a man of the land whereas, when she'd bumped into him, in a grey suit, he'd definitely been more of a high-flying businessman.

She shivered involuntarily. He'd been so angry in a quiet but deadly sort of way.

'Talk to me, Harriet,' he said firmly.

She took a sip of tea and then a deep breath. 'I need a job, quite urgently.'

'You—according to Arthur, anyway—are highly, if not to say über-qualified. Why would you want my job?' He frowned. 'It's stuck out in the country even if you don't have an army of lovers to worry about.'

'It…' Harriet paused '…suits me.'

'Why?'

A short silence developed between them and lengthened until he said impatiently, 'Oh, come on Harriet! I—'

'I just want to get this job,' she said with sudden intensity, 'on my merits.'

'Well, your merits are fine but I need to know more,' he said flatly.

'This kind of job doesn't grow on trees,' Harriet said after a long moment. 'And it so happens it's the right district for me.'

'Why?'

Harriet sighed. 'My brother was badly injured in a surfing accident. He's now in a rehabilitation centre at—' she named a facility '—that's handy to Lennox Head and Heathcote. He has to learn to walk again. That's why—' she looked up at last and smiled with considerable irony '—when this job came up, it seemed like an answer to all my prayers. Until, that was—' She stopped abruptly.

'You found out whose job it was,' Damien supplied.

She didn't answer but looked away.

'You decided to proceed, however.' It was a statement, not a question.

'Yes.'

'And I suppose that's why you wanted to make sure the weekends were free? So you could see your brother. Talk about coals of fire,' he murmured wryly. He added impatiently, 'Why couldn't you have just told me all this in the first place?'

Harriet shrugged. 'Ever since I found out about the job, I've been…I have been a nervous wreck,' she conceded. She gestured. 'It would be so perfect but…' She shrugged again. 'To be perfectly honest, you're the last person I would want to accept a favour from.'

He grimaced. 'Needs must when the devil drives. You need the money?'

'I need the money,' she agreed rather dryly. 'This is a private hospital and it's not covered by my brother's medical insurance but it has a terrific reputation. And to be able to be close to Brett at the same time is an obvious bonus.'

'I see. Has it—' he paused and raised an eyebrow at her '—occurred to you that I was simply driving along minding my own business that day when all hell erupted, in a manner of speaking?'

She cast him a dark little look from beneath her lashes. 'Accidents happen.'

'Yes, but I thought you might be able to cut me a little slack—no, I see not,' he murmured as her lips set.

And, he continued, but to himself, you not only have amazingly long eyelashes, Harriet Livingstone, but a rather gorgeous mouth, severely sculptured yet somehow incredibly inviting. Plus—he allowed his dark gaze to roam over her—satiny-smooth skin, slender delicate wrists and lovely hands that I quite failed to notice the last time we met.

So that's it, Damien Wyatt, he castigated himself inwardly. Even with all the things you didn't notice then, this damn girl made an impression on you two months ago and that's why you felt goaded into seeing her again. What's more, she's making even more of an impression on you today, which is not going to lead *anywhere*, he told himself grimly.

But how to knock her back for the job?

In all decency you can't, he decided. So what to do if she keeps on making an impression on you?

A dry smile briefly twisted his lips—think of your poor car before it got fixed…

'Well, you've got the job if you want it,' he said abruptly. 'Would you like to see the studio and flat before you make up your mind?'

Harriet clenched her hands in her lap. 'You don't have to feel sorry for me,' she said carefully. 'When one door closes another usually opens.'

'Harriet,' he warned, 'I don't appreciate being told what I should or should not feel but, if you want to get it right, I don't only feel sorry for you—most people would in the circumstances—but I feel as guilty as hell for the things I said over what was, you're right, an accident.'

'Oh...'

'Now, could we get *on* with it? You've barely had a drop of your tea,' he added with sudden frustration.

Harriet grabbed her purse. 'I'll leave it.'

She got up so precipitously, she tripped over Tottie and would have fallen to the floor if Damien hadn't lunged forward and caught her.

The next moments were confused as he untangled her from the dog, the coffee table and she ended up standing in the middle of the room in his arms.

'You wouldn't be accident-prone, would you?' he asked incredulously.

Harriet tried to free herself but, although he held her quite loosely, he made it plain he was not about to let her go. 'I…I suffer from a left-handed syndrome,' she said a little raggedly.

'What the hell's that?'

'My father's invention to explain the fact that I'm a bit uncoordinated at times.'

'So, yes—' he raised his eyebrows '—acci-dent prone?'

She shrugged. 'Maybe. Would you mind let-ting me go?'

Damien Wyatt still had a spark of amusement in his eyes as he said wryly, 'Yes I would, heaven alone knows why. Well, for one thing I've never held a girl as tall as you but it feels good.'

'I…' Harriet opened her mouth to protest but he lowered his head and started to kiss her.

Shock seemed to take away all her powers of resistance and when he lifted his head she could only stare up at him with her eyes wide, her lips still parted and her heart beating heavily.

'Mmm…' He ran his hands up and down her back and hugged her. 'I must have been mad ever to think you were skinny, Ms Livingstone!'

Harriet gathered herself. 'This is…this is,' she started to say.

'Insane?' he supplied.

'*Yes*,' she agreed, almost biting her tongue in her frustration.

'You're not wrong. On the other hand, we've experienced quite a range of emotions—'

'That's—what's that got to do with it?' Harriet broke in desperately.

'We've been angry with each other,' he went on.

'You murderously,' she pointed out darkly.

'Well, not quite, but you've hated my guts,' he responded. 'I reckon we're destined to run through the whole spectrum—you know, your eyes are stunning.'

'I...they...'

'And there's your skin.' He transferred his hands to her arms and ran his palms down them. 'Smooth and satiny. As for your legs—by the way, I wouldn't ever wear that wraparound skirt again...' He paused as she moved convulsively and waited for her to quieten before he went on. 'Only because it's criminal to hide your legs.'

'Mr Wyatt,' Harriet said through her teeth, 'please don't go on and will you let me go!'

'In a minute. The other thing Arthur was right about; you have a slightly superior edge at times.'

Harriet, about to make a concerted effort to free herself, stopped dead and stared at him, completely mystified. 'What do you mean?'

'Well, for example, in the lounge earlier,' he elucidated, 'you looked at me as if I'd crawled out from under a rock.'

'I did not!' she denied.

'You probably don't realise you're doing it. Actually, what Arthur said was that you sometimes look as if your mind is on higher things.'

Harriet blinked. 'What does that mean?'

He dropped his arms and moved back half a pace but Harriet stayed where she was. 'That you think you're above this "mortal coil"?' he mused, and shrugged. 'Perhaps way above the sweaty realities of life and love, not to mention men? You did say there was no one. One has to wonder why.' He stopped and shrugged.

Harriet Livingstone very rarely lost her temper but when she did the consequences were often disastrous, mainly because she was tall enough to be effective about it. She advanced the half step towards Damien Wyatt and slapped his face. She did more.

'Oh, how I've wanted to do that,' she gasped but with great passion. 'Talk about being above the mortal coil—*you* obviously see yourself as the bee's knees!'

His lips twisted as he fingered his cheek.

'Bee's knees—haven't heard that one for a while. All the same, Stretch,' he responded, 'I—'

'*Don't* call me that,' she warned.

'Whatever.' He shrugged and took her in his arms and proceeded to kiss her again but this time there was a definite purpose to it. This time it was a battle, not a shocked passive response on her part and a more light-hearted exploration on his.

Until he lifted his head and said abruptly, 'No, no more anger and hate, Harriet.'

'What do you mean?'

'It's time to move on. No, don't do a thing, I'm not going to hurt you, it's just that fate seems to have intervened.' He shook his head. 'It certainly has for me.'

And this time, before he kissed her again, he drew her into his body and ran his hands over her in a way that made her go still and her eyes widen in a different kind of shock because it was as if he was imparting an electric current through her, a tide of sensuality she couldn't resist.

Then he released her and cupped her face in his hands and they looked into each other's eyes for a long, long moment. And as she breathed in the essence of Damien Wyatt it had a powerful effect on her. Not only did he bring the outdoors into the dining room—there were sweat stains on his shirt, his hair was ruffled—but a physical force and the aroma of pure man.

Then, as she searched his dark eyes and saw the way they were focused on her and felt the way his hands moved down to her hips and were gentle but skilful on her body, she got a different sense of him.

As if she was viewing the man behind the man. As if, underneath that prickly, easily prone to irritation exterior, there was a man who knew how to make love to a woman in a way that thrilled her and drove her to excesses she hadn't known she could reach…

And when he started to kiss her again, because of that sense of him, because of the rapturous tingling of all her senses, something she'd been denied for a long time, because of the feel of the hard planes of his body against her, because he was actually taller than she was and because there was something terribly, awe-inspiringly masculine about him unless you were a block of wood, she found herself kissing him back.

They drew apart briefly once. They were both breathing raggedly. He pulled the ribbon out of her hair and ran his fingers through it. She spread her fingers on his back and felt the sleek strength of it beneath his shirt.

Then he was kissing her again and her breasts were crushed against him as he held her hard.

It was the dining room door opening and a spontaneous whistle that brought Harriet Livingstone and Damien Wyatt back to earth.

Not that Damien betrayed any sign of discomfort, at first.

He released her in a leisurely way and tidied the collar of her dress before he said over her shoulder, 'Charlie, this is Harriet Livingstone. Harriet—' he put his hands on her shoulders

'—it's OK. Meet my brother, Charles Walker Wyatt. He's renowned for rushing in where angels fear to tread.'

Harriet swallowed and put her hands up to try to tidy her hair before she forced herself to turn around.

Charles Walker Wyatt wasn't as tall as his brother Damien and he looked to be several years younger. He also bore an arrested expression on his face, as of one who had received a smack on the head when least expecting it.

'Holy…Mackerel, Damien!' he exclaimed then. 'The last thing I expected to find in the *dining room* of all places was you kissing a girl I've never laid eyes on! That's hardly *fools rushing in* material—wouldn't you agree, ma'am?' he appealed to Harriet as he advanced towards them.

'By the way, please forgive me,' he went on, 'for labelling you "a girl"—not that you're *not* but it sounds sort of generic and I don't mean to classify you like that. Not at all! But—'

'Charlie.' There was a definite warning note in Damien's voice.

'Damien?' Charlie replied, looking innocent. 'Just tell me what I'm allowed to say and do and I'll try not to put a foot wrong!'

'What anyone with a grain of courtesy or good sense would have done in the first place,' his brother replied evenly. 'Retreated and shut the flaming door!'

The last bit was said a little less than evenly and it struck Harriet that Damien Wyatt was not completely unaffected by his brother's intrusion.

'Ah.' Charlie rubbed his chin. 'OK—but actually, I've had a better idea. What's wrong with me getting to know Miss Harriet Livingstone?' And he looked admiringly at Harriet.

'Everything,' Damien snapped. 'Just go away, Charlie!' he added, his irritation and rising impatience plain to be seen.

Something Charles Walker Wyatt obviously saw for himself because he sketched a salute, did a military about-turn and said, 'Just going, sir.' He marched out smartly.

Damien waited until the door closed before turning back to Harriet. 'Do you know something?' he said bitterly. 'Every time we get within cooee of each other, you and I, it turns out to be a shambles!'

Harriet swallowed. 'I think I should just go. It could never work.'

'*Go*?' he said through his teeth, 'How the hell can you kiss a guy like that and just go?'

CHAPTER TWO

'YOU STARTED IT,' Harriet said and immediately despised herself for sounding incredibly lame and childish. 'I mean…' But she found it impossible to sort out her thoughts let alone her emotions.

'If you hadn't tripped over the damn dog, I might not have started it,' he replied irritably. 'Anyway! How come Tottie is so taken with you?'

'I don't know.' Harriet shrugged helplessly. 'Dogs do just seem to take to me.'

'Look—' he studied her '—sit down and have another cup of tea—no, I'll pour it—hang on, I've got a better idea.' He guided her to a chair at the dining table and pulled it out for her. 'Sit down and study some of my mother's incomparable collection; it might calm you. While I pour us a drink.'

He turned away towards a cocktail cabinet.

Harriet drew a deep breath and combed her hair with her fingers but she couldn't find her ribbon so she had to leave it loose. She took a hanky out of her purse and patted her face. Then her attention was drawn to an exquisite cameo in an old-fashioned rose-gold and pin-point diamond setting and she forgot about the wreck she might look as she stared at it rapturously. And Damien Wyatt put a glass of brandy down beside her and pulled out a chair opposite to sit down with his own drink.

'Cheers,' he said.

Harriet hesitated.

'Don't think about it; just drink it,' he advised.

So she took a couple of sips and felt the brandy slip down and a warm glow of—what was it? Some confidence?—rise in its place.

But, before she could formulate anything sensible to say, he spoke. 'How well do you know Arthur?'

'Hardly at all. I know Penny better. We were at college together for a while, although she's a few years older. Then we lost track of each other until I came up to Ballina. It was quite an amazing coincidence. I literally bumped into her—no,' she said with her lips quirking suddenly as his eyebrows flew up, 'not the way I bumped into you. This was on the pavement as we were walking along.'

A gleam of amusement lit his eyes. 'I'm relieved to hear you say so. Go on.'

She looked rueful. 'So we had coffee and compared notes. She told me about Arthur and how they'd moved from Sydney to Ballina to get out of the rat race. She told me she'd started a picture-framing business and a small art gallery and how Arthur still dealt in art—he was born up here apparently.'

'Yes. He was a friend of my father's; more than that, he helped Dad establish his collection.'

'So I told her I'd also decided to get away from the rat race and I was looking for a job. That's when she grew thoughtful and finally dragged me off to meet Arthur.'

'I see.' Damien swirled the liquid in his glass. 'So they didn't know—' he lifted his dark gaze to her '—about your brother?'

'No.' Harriet traced the rim of her glass with her forefinger then took another sip. 'I know it seems a bit deceitful, but I find it hard to deal with people feeling sorry for us.'

He was silent for a time, then, 'What were you doing up here two months ago, when you bumped into me?'

'I was checking out this rehabilitation centre. It was the first time I'd been to this area—another reason I was a bit dithery, I guess; I didn't know my way around.'

'It's not exactly a metropolis,' he said wryly then gestured as if to delete the comment. 'But you're living up here now? Your brother's in the rehab centre?'

Harriet nodded.

'Where are you living?'

She hesitated then took a sip of the brandy and shrugged. 'In a rented caravan in the caravan park. I do have a job—it's waitressing, so it keeps the wolf from the door, but—' She broke off.

'Only just?' he suggested.

She didn't respond but stared a bit blindly down at her glass.

'OK,' he said quietly, 'no more interrogations. The job is yours if you want it but what are we going to do?'

'Do?' she repeated.

He set his teeth. 'Yes, do! About the rest of it?'

Her deep blue eyes widened. 'The rest of it?'

He grimaced. 'You must have a short memory span as well as being accident-prone. Or do you often go around kissing guys like that?'

The confidence she'd got from a few sips of brandy ebbed a little at the same time as her eyes widened as the full memory of their passionate encounter hit her.

She took a larger mouthful of brandy.

'You had forgotten,' he marvelled.

'No. But we did get interrupted,' she responded tartly. 'I don't know about you, but I found it extremely embarrassing. Enough to make the rest of it, well…' She broke off as she searched for the right words.

'Pale into insignificance?' he suggested dryly.

'Not exactly,' Harriet denied and took another sip of her drink. 'But it did—move it back a bit if you know what I mean.' She paused and shrugged. 'It probably put it into its right perspective.'

'What would that be?'

She glinted him an assessing look from beneath her lashes, then thought—why should I try to spare his feelings? 'It was just something that happened in the heat of the moment, wasn't it?'

'Go on.'

Harriet hesitated, unable to read his expression

but feeling a prickle of apprehension run through her. 'Well, you insulted me, I responded—'

'With a blow, allow me to remind you.' He looked sardonically amused.

Harriet compressed her lips. 'I'm sorry. I believe I had cause, however. Look—' she paused '—I wouldn't be surprised if you weren't still furious with me over your car.'

'Not to mention my collarbone. There are still some things I can't do. I'm not still furious, however.' Damien Wyatt crossed his arms and leant back with a frown growing in his dark eyes. 'Well, I may have been a bit annoyed but I have to say I'm mostly confused now. In fact I'm beginning to wonder if I'm hallucinating. Did you or did you not kiss me back almost like a woman starved for—that kind of thing?'

Harriet stared at the cameo for a long moment then looked at him squarely. 'Maybe. But it's best forgotten.'

'Why?'

Harriet pushed her glass away and stood up.

'Because I have no intention of getting involved with you, Mr Wyatt. Please don't take that personally. I'm…I'm…happy to be fancy-free, that's all.'

He stared at her and she was suddenly conscious that not only was she completely unable to read his thoughts but, more than that, it troubled her.

Why? Why should she care one way or another about what he thought of her? The sensual response he'd managed to draw from her had come about because he was experienced and worldly—she had little doubt of that—so why should she invest it with any special meaning or depth?

Well, she amended her thoughts, she had to take some responsibility for her reaction, surely? Starved? Perhaps—but she didn't even want to think about that…

'Would you mind if I went now? I'm sorry if I've wasted your time but I honestly don't think it could work.'

Damien stayed absolutely still for a moment longer then he straightened and stood up, leaning his fists on the table. 'Yes, I would mind,' he said dryly, 'and I'll tell you why. I don't propose to have you on my conscience for a moment longer, whether I realise it or not, Harriet Livingstone.'

'You don't have to have me on your conscience!' she objected.

'Believe me, I'd rather not but—'

'What do you mean—whether you realise it or not?' Harriet broke in to ask with a frown.

He shrugged. 'I can't work out why else I agreed to see you again.'

Harriet linked her fingers together and told herself not to pursue this but some demon prompted her, rather than simply getting up and walking out, to say, 'If you think I could ever work for you, you must be mad, Mr Wyatt.'

Their gazes clashed.

'The job is yours, Miss Livingstone,' he replied deliberately. 'You can move in the day after tomorrow—I'll be gone then. I'm going overseas for some weeks, at least a month. Of course Isabel, who runs the house and the rest of it when I'm not here, will be in residence. So will Charlie, for a while anyway. Did Arthur get around to mentioning the remuneration package we thought was suitable?'

Harriet blinked. '...Yes.'

'You can add a twenty per cent commission on any items I decide to sell. Will that do?'

'I...I...' She hesitated.

'Don't go all dithery on me again, Harriet,' he warned. 'Finish your brandy,' he ordered.

She stared at him, deep hostility written into her expression. 'No. I've got to drive.'

'All right, but I need to know if you're going to take it or not.'

Harriet would have given the world to answer in the negative but if he was going to be away... and surely she could finish the job in a month if she worked day and night...?

'I'll take it,' she said barely audibly.

'Do you want to see the studio and the flat?'

'No.' She shook her head. 'I'm sure they'll be fine.'

He studied her narrowly with a glint of curiosity in his dark eyes. 'I can't work out if you're a superior, head-in-the-clouds although accident-prone academic type or a rather exotic bundle of nerves.'

Harriet took a breath and actually managed to smile. 'If it's any help, neither can I. Goodbye, Tottie,' she added and patted the dog's head.

Damien Wyatt looked heavenwards as Tottie came as close as such a regal-looking dog could to actually simpering.

At the same time, Harriet said, 'Oh! I wonder where I put my glasses?'

'Here,' he remarked flatly, picking them up from the dining table and handing them to her. 'I'll see you out.'

Harriet hesitated. 'I'm sure I could see myself out.'

'Not at all. After you.'

So it was that Harriet preceded him out of the dining room and out of the house to the driveway. There was only one vehicle parked there: hers.

Damien Wyatt took one look at it and swore. 'You're not still driving that damn tank, are you?' he asked with furious incredulity.

Harriet coloured slightly. 'It just refuses to lie down. Anyway, it's not mine, it's Brett's, my brother's. It's very good over rough and sandy terrain.'

'I believe you.' Damien favoured the vehicle with a lingering look of malice then transferred his gaze to Harriet.

'Well, enjoy your stay at Heathcote, Miss Livingstone.' A tinge of irony entered his dark eyes. 'Don't go about kissing too many men at the same time as you're happy to remain fancy-free. Oh, and watch out for Charlie. He is, not to put too fine a point on it, a womaniser.'

Harriet drew a deep breath. 'Perhaps he takes

after you?' she said quietly, and climbed into her battered old vehicle.

He waited until she'd driven off before saying to Tottie, 'What the devil do you make of all that? OK, I know you're on *her* side, but I don't ever recall kissing a girl I've—virtually—just met like that.'

Predictably, Tottie didn't answer; she only yawned.

Damien Wyatt shrugged. In fact I haven't kissed anyone quite like that for a while, he added to himself. Been too busy, been somewhat cynical about the whole tribe of women, to be honest. What I need, if that's the case, is someone nice and uncomplicated who knows the rules of the game—doesn't expect wedding bells in other words—rather than importuning an accident-prone, scholarly type who drives a horrible vehicle and has the nerve to suborn my dog!

'That's you, Tottie,' he said severely but Tottie remained serenely unaffected.

'Of course you could always kind of…keep an eye on her while I'm away,' Damien added. 'Heaven knows what "a left-handed syndrome" could lead her into.'

'Permission to speak,' a voice said and Charlie strolled onto the drive.

'Don't start, Charlie,' Damien advised.

'She's gone, I see.' Charlie came to a stop beside Tottie and his brother. He shoved his hands into his pockets. 'Unusual vehicle. For a girl, I mean. Not to mention some kind of an antique dealer, according to Isabel.'

'It's her brother's, apparently. Listen, Charlie—' he explained Harriet's background and the agreement they'd reached '—so leave her alone, will you?'

Charlie looked offended. 'Acquit me! Would I try to steal your girl?'

'Yes,' Damien said flatly. 'Not that *she's* my girl—not that she's *my* girl—' He broke off and swore. 'But she's got a job to do here and the sooner it's done, the better.'

Charlie frowned. 'Why do I sense a mystery attached to Miss Harriet Livingstone? Smashing pair of legs, by the way.'

'I don't know,' Damien said shortly. 'How long are you here for?'

'Relax, Bro,' Charlie said cheerfully. 'I'm due back at the base in a week. By the way, you are now talking to Flight Lieutenant Charles Walker Wyatt. Which is what I dashed into the dining room to tell you, incidentally.'

'Charlie!' Damien turned to his brother. 'Congratulations!' And he shook his brother's hand then enveloped him in a bear hug.

'I suspect I got it by the skin of my teeth but, yeah!'

'Come in and I'll shout you a drink.'

It was just before they were called into dinner that Charlie said thoughtfully, 'There's something about that girl, Damien. Easy to run onto the rocks there—take care.'

Damien Wyatt opened his mouth to deny that

there was any possibility of his running onto any rocks with Harriet Livingstone but he closed it.

And he said musingly, 'I'm glad to hear you say so because for the last few hours I've been wondering what on earth got into me. So what do you think it is?'

Charlie shook his head. 'I don't know,' he said. 'But some women just have an aura of…reserve, maybe, with a dash of vulnerability, a tinge of heartbreak perhaps, and that—' he waved his tankard '—certain something you just can't put into words.'

'That *je ne sais quoi*,' Damien murmured. He frowned. 'And you sensed all this about Harriet Livingstone in—roughly two minutes?'

Charlie looked wise. 'I once decided to date a girl I saw riding past me on a bicycle. All I saw was the curve of her cheek and all this shiny brown hair floating out behind her but it was enough. I chased her in my car, persuaded her to pop the bike in the boot and have lunch with me. We dated for quite a few months.'

'What broke it up?' Damien enquired curiously.

'The Air Force. I didn't get to spend enough time with her. Anyway, getting back to you. After Veronica, well…' Charlie shrugged as if he didn't quite know how to go on.

'Veronica,' Damien repeated expressionlessly.

'Your ex-wife,' Charlie explained generously. 'Gorgeous girl, of course, but—tricky.'

Damien raised his eyebrows. 'Good at hiding it, though.'

'Met her match when she ran into you, *however*,' Charlie declaimed. 'I—'

'Charlie,' Damien said gently, 'the only reason I've let the discussion get this far is because I'm feeling rather mellow on account of your promotion but that's enough.'

'Right-ho! Just don't say I didn't warn you!'

'Isn't that the guy you ran into?'

Brett Livingstone sat in a wheelchair in his

pleasant room in the rehabilitation centre but his expression was troubled.

Harriet sat in an armchair opposite. She'd come straight from Heathcote with the news of the job she'd got—she hadn't told her brother anything about it before in case it hadn't come off.

'Yes. But that's all in the past and it's not only what I love doing, it comes with accommodation.'

'Are you safe with him?'

'Safe?' Harriet stared at him. 'Of course.'

Brett looked angry. 'He sounded like a thug and a bully.'

Harriet bit her lip. 'It was a very beautiful car. But look; his aunt lives there. So does his brother from time to time, and there's staff. And he has this marvellous dog. Her name's Tottie and she's very highly bred.'

Brett smiled reluctantly as he studied his sister's bright expression. 'Any kind of a dog could get you in, Harry.'

She grimaced. 'I suppose so. But really, Brett, it's the kind of job most people who do what I do would dream about. And—' she hesitated, wishing fervently she'd never told her brother about running into Damien Wyatt '—I'm not a very good waitress,' she added humorously. 'Can I stay and have dinner with you?'

'Sure. Hey—' Brett sat forward '—how can I ever thank you?'

Harriet had never lived in a caravan before but several weeks of it now had convinced her she wasn't cut out to be a gypsy.

Despite the fact that the van was clean and modern, she felt claustrophobic and found it hard to sleep. Of course her state of mind for the last few months hadn't helped.

Lennox Head was situated in the Northern Rivers District of New South Wales. Not on a river itself, it lay between the Tweed and Richmond Rivers, and as well as a distinctive headland that attracted surfers from around the world and hang-gliders too, it had a marvellous seven-mile beach.

Inland, the country was green, fertile and undulating until it came up against the Border Ranges. Sugar was grown on the coastal flats; coffee and custard apples amongst others further inland but the biggest crop of the district was macadamia nuts. It was pleasant country, home to huge camphor laurel trees and many colourful shrubs.

When she got back to the van, Harriet changed and went for a brisk walk then came back and sat on a bench.

It was a quiet evening.

She could hear the surf, she could see stars, but she had no sense of freedom.

And she still had Brett on her mind…

At twenty, he was six years younger than she was and their mother had passed away when he was a baby. Looking after and worrying about her little brother had been a way of life for Harriet for as long as she could remember.

For that matter, looking after their father was something she'd done as she'd got older. Until his death a couple of years ago, he'd been a delightful person, humorous, always devising little surprises for his children, telling them marvellous stories but otherwise quite hopeless when it came to the mundane things of life like saving and planning for the future.

Therefore they'd lived from day to day to a certain extent—when work was plentiful it was a lobster month he'd used to say, when it wasn't plentiful, mince on toast. And they'd moved a lot between capital cities and major and minor art galleries.

However, it was thanks to her father that Harriet had acquired much of her knowledge of antiques and art. She'd shared his fascination for them and some of her earliest memories were of visits with him to art galleries and art auctions, memories of reading art history books with him.

Brett couldn't have been more different. Athletic and with a love of the sea, he'd decided on a career as a professional surfer. And he'd been slowly making a name for himself when he'd been struck down by a freak accident and for a while no one had expected him to walk again.

But he was—just, if you could even call the sweat-soaked, painful inch by inch progress that.

But at least, Harriet mused, he was getting the best treatment now, and she had enough resources to ensure this treatment was maintained.

Which led her thoughts onto the subject of Damien Wyatt and the incredible turn of events of the afternoon.

A tremor ran through her as she remembered being in his arms and the powerfully sensual effect he'd had on her.

How could she have been so affected? she wondered. Was it simply the human contact and warmth she'd responded to?

It had to be something like that because hadn't she sworn never to fall in love again?

She grimaced at how melodramatic it sounded and wondered suddenly if she did project a neu-

rotic image. And how about scholarly or academic as well as accident-prone? Superior?

Or how about just plain lonely?

She bit her lip and blinked away a sudden tear.

CHAPTER THREE

TWO WEEKS LATER, memories of her time in the caravan had started to fade and she'd fitted into the Heathcote lifestyle easily.

The flat above the converted stable block was comfortable and self-contained. It had a galley-style kitchen with all mod cons that appealed to Harriet. She was a keen and innovative cook and it wasn't long before she had a variety of herbs growing in pots on the windowsills. There was a rather lovely old wooden refectory table with benches.

The lounge area had comfortable armchairs and a view of the sea. The one bedroom was home to a king-sized bed, the lightest, warmest quilts and was rather sumptuously decorated in shades of violet and thyme-green.

Isabel had confessed to being the decorator and also to having gone a bit overboard in the bedroom.

Isabel was becoming friendlier and friendlier. She was Damien and Charlie's father's sister; she'd never married and it was plain to see that she ran not only the house but the estate with a lot of care and affection. She'd confided to Harriet once that she knew every inch of the estate and every nook of the house because she'd not only grown up at Heathcote but spent most of her life there.

She certainly handled the small army of staff required—gardeners, cleaners, stable hands and one highly temperamental cook—with ease. Well, she'd confessed to Harriet that she suspected the cook, a Queenslander, was not only temperamental but that he drank and she really should sack him but he claimed to have six children under ten. He also cooked like an angel...

It hadn't required much insight on Harriet's part to see that Isabel doted on her nephews.

And she very early on discovered that Isabel always carried out Damien's instructions.

This discovery came, in fact, on the day Harriet arrived to take up residence at Heathcote. Isabel came up to the flat that afternoon to see how Harriet had settled in and at the same time she handed over a set of car keys.

Harriet looked at the keys with a frown. 'What are these for?'

'There's a blue Holden in the garage. It's not new but it's in great condition. It's for you to use while you're here. In fact, if you give me your car keys, I'll get your vehicle parked elsewhere.'

'Do I…do I detect the hand of Damien Wyatt here?' Harriet said ominously.

Isabel grimaced. 'You do.'

'Well, if he thinks he can—'

'I've been told to let you go if you don't agree to the Holden,' Isabel interrupted, and patted Harriet's arm. 'Much easier to drive, I'm sure. Besides, there's something about your vehicle that—upsets Damien.'

'I can understand that, but Damien is not here,' Harriet pointed out to his aunt.

'Damien is always here,' Isabel remarked with some irony. 'He seems to have a sixth sense about the place even if he's a million miles away. Please?' she added.

Harriet breathed deeply. 'If you must know, I can't help thinking he's a bit of a control freak!'

'Oh, definitely!' Isabel agreed. 'More than a bit, in fact. But it was—' she put her head on one side '—rather a thoughtful thing to do, don't you think?'

Harriet pursed her lips. 'I suppose so,' she said at length, and flinched inwardly a little to hear herself repeating the bit about it being *rather a thoughtful thing to do* to Brett that evening when she drove over in the blue Holden to see him.

'Thoughtful?' Brett repeated as she wheeled him out to the car park to look at it. 'You sure the guy's not sweet on you, Harry?'

'Quite s...' Harriet paused then said hastily, 'I

think *your* car keeps reminding him of what I did to his beloved Aston Martin with it.'

'But he's not here to see it,' Brett objected.

'He has eyes in the back of his head—or something like that,' Harriet said gloomily, then forced herself to brighten up. 'How's it going?'

'I've got a new physio,' Brett replied. 'She's really cool. I'm walking a wee bit further every day.'

Harriet narrowed her eyes as she picked up a jaunty note she hadn't heard in her brother's voice for a long time. And she found herself crossing her fingers metaphorically and sending up a little prayer at the same time that this 'she', this new physio, might just be the one to provide her brother with the spark he needed.

The other aspect of life at Heathcote, of course, was Charlie. He didn't spend a lot of time on the estate during his furlough but when he did he always popped in to see Harriet.

It was probably during the third such visit that

Harriet confirmed what she'd first suspected—
that Charles Walker Wyatt treated her in rather
a strange manner.

And she couldn't help mentioning it at the
same time as she couldn't keep a straight face.
'Charlie,' she said with a chuckle, 'do I look as
if I've popped down from Mars?'

'Mars,' he repeated, looking startled. He was
lounging at the refectory table eating an apple
plucked from her bowl when he wasn't watching her in that curiously assessing way he had.
'What makes you say that?'

'You have a way of looking at me and sort
of…testing everything I say as if it has a hidden
meaning or *I* have something about me you just
don't understand.'

'Ah.' Charlie took a large bite of his apple.
'Well…' He munched and thought. 'I've never
met anyone quite like you, I guess.'

He paused and studied her thoughtfully. She
wore tight black shorts and a sapphire-blue tank
top. Her hair was bunched up on top of her head

and she wore her red-rimmed glasses as she studied a recipe she was planning to make for her dinner. It was an unexceptional outfit by any standards and yet it emphasised how trim and slim her figure was, how long her legs were.

No wonder Damien had got a bit carried away, Charlie found himself thinking as Harriet reached up and took down a pottery casserole dish.

Even used as he is to the crème de la crème, there's certainly something, well, subtly, but all the same eye-catching about Ms Harriet Livingstone, Charlie thought. Why on earth did I promise to leave her alone…?

'Charlie?'

He came out of his thoughts to find Harriet staring at him. 'Uh—I've certainly never met anyone who works as hard as you do. You were still working at midnight when I got home last night!'

'That's because I'd like to finish this project before your brother gets—' She stopped abruptly.

'Before Damien gets home? Why?' he asked simply.

Harriet shrugged.

'His bark is a lot worse than his bite, as I should know.'

'It may be but I...' She paused.

'And you certainly must have made quite an impression on him because, believe me,' Charlie said earnestly, 'he's usually intensely private about his affairs. I got put firmly in my place only a couple of weeks ago when all I did was mention Veronica's name. She's his ex-wife,' he added obligingly, and waited.

I will not rise to the bait, Harriet vowed.

'So am I—very private,' she said shortly then relented as Charlie's expression became wounded. 'Look, it was just one of those... things. He got furious with me over the accident. I got furious with him because I thought he was arrogant and high-handed and it all seemed to blow up again into—' She stopped and took a breath then said laconically, 'If I hadn't slapped his face I wouldn't have got myself so thoroughly kissed.'

'Slapped his face!' Charlie was wide-eyed and incredulously admiring.

'Yes,' Harriet replied shortly. 'Not that I'm proud of it, but he did call me Stretch, which is something I can't abide. And that is the last word I intend to say on the matter. So, off you go, Charlie, please. I need to concentrate on this recipe.'

The studio that had been converted from stables was a pleasure to work in. There was plenty of light, plenty of bench space, a lot of shelving, a sink, even a microscope as well as a computer.

But, of course, the other thing that made Harriet feel at home was Tottie's presence. The big dog became her constant companion. They went for walks together. They went down to the beach and they visited the stables together, where Harriet made special friends with one of the horses, a bubbly grey mare that went by the name of Sprite.

Stan, the stable foreman, offered to let her ride Sprite, if she rode, which she had as a child, but she declined and contented herself with taking the mare carrots every evening.

And there were other times when Harriet caught herself talking to Tottie as if she were human.

She'd wondered how Isabel would take this but it only amused her. 'She's always been Damien's dog,' she told Harriet, 'but of course he's away a lot so she doesn't get to see that much of him.'

So far as the business side of her stay at Heathcote went, one thing Harriet had insisted on was a system whereby all of Damien's mother's treasures were dual-catalogued. In other words, Isabel handled them first, kept her own record, then handed them over to Harriet.

'Did you think we'd not trust you?' Isabel had

asked curiously when Harriet had suggested the scheme. 'You come so highly recommended.'

'It's always better to be safe rather than sorry,' Harriet had replied. 'This way we're both pro- tected.'

And Arthur, who drove up from Ballina oc- casionally, agreed.

Three weeks after she'd arrived at Heathcote, it was a glorious summer's day and she and Tottie went down to the beach. No one else was home. Charlie had gone back to his base and Isabel, who sat on several committees, was in Lismore helping to co-ordinate a charity drive and was spending the night with a friend.

They were the only ones on the beach, she and Tottie, and they frolicked in the surf and played with a ball until finally Harriet called out that she had to get back to work.

But something else had engaged the dog's at- tention after she'd dropped the ball at Harriet's feet. She stiffened, growled low in her throat and then took off like a shaggy arrow in full flight.

Harriet turned and discovered there was a man standing beside her towel where she'd dropped it on the grass verge above the beach—a man Tottie obviously knew because she skidded to a halt in front of him, barked with obvious joy this time, and leapt up to lay her paws on his shoulders—Damien Wyatt.

Harriet froze. Then she swallowed nervously as their last encounter and the last thing she'd said to him, the insult she'd offered him, stood out clearly in her mind.

Plus, even from further down the beach she could see he was wearing a suit, just as he had the day of the accident when he'd been so angry.

She hesitated and looked down at herself. Her lemon and lime flowered bikini was reasonably modest but it was still a bikini and she would have much rather been wearing a boilersuit or a combat uniform with all its paraphernalia for this encounter.

There was nothing for it, however, than to stroll up the beach, to say hi as casually as she could and to pick up her towel and wrap it around her. Perhaps then she could say something along the lines of *You're home early!* or *Welcome home! I have enjoyed Heathcote—* Stop it! she commanded herself. Just do it…!

It was a nerve-racking trudge up the beach but, when she was halfway there, Tottie came prancing back to her with delight written into her movements and a smile on her doggy face.

In fact Harriet had to grin in spite of herself, so infectious was the dog's enthusiasm.

'Hello, Damien,' she said as she reached him, almost confident that Tottie had eased the situation for her. She certainly didn't trip or fall as she picked up her towel and wrapped it around her sarong-wise but then she glanced up at him and things changed.

He wore a grey suit with a white shirt and a dark blue tie but he'd loosened his tie and unbuttoned the top button of his shirt. His hands were shoved into his trouser pockets.

And it struck Harriet like a blow to her heart that she'd fooled herself over the past weeks. Fooled herself into believing she'd completely rationalised the effect Damien had had on her.

More than that; she'd buried herself in his mother's treasures and convinced herself she wasn't even thinking of him. Only to know now that he'd been there on the back roads of her mind all the time; he must have been because every intimate detail of the passionate encounter they'd shared came back to her.

Not only did they come back to her but they trapped her into immobility, with her breathing growing ragged and her senses stirring as she stared at him and thought of the feel of his tall body against hers, the delight his hands had wrought on her.

Trapped her staring at him as a sea breeze lifted his dark hair off his forehead and brought her out in goose bumps—was it the breeze or was it part of the effect he was having on her, so she couldn't speak, she couldn't tear her eyes away?

Then she noticed he was watching her just as intently and there was a muscle flickering in his jaw that told a tale of its own as his gaze slid down to her legs, barely hidden under the towel.

Tottie came to the rescue. She bunted them both playfully, as if to say—*Come on, you two, don't just stand there!*

Harriet had to relax a little and smile. So did Damien.

He also said, 'I hope my dog has been taking good care of you?'

'She's been a very faithful friend these last couple of weeks.' Harriet squeezed out her hair. 'I didn't know you were coming home.'

'No.' His dark eyes lingered on her figure and her legs again below the towel. 'Something came up unexpectedly. You look…well.'

Harriet smoothed the towel. 'Thanks.' Her

voice was husky and she cleared her throat. 'So do you.'

A smile appeared fleetingly in his eyes. 'We sound like a mutual admiration society, a stilted one at that. But anyway, how's your brother?'

He turned and indicated they walk up to the house.

'He's making good progress and I've enrolled him as an external student at the Southern Cross University in Lismore.'

'What subject?'

She grimaced. 'Sports Psychology. I was hoping to wean him away from that kind of thing but—no go.'

'Better than nothing—a lot better,' Damien commented.

'Yes—ouch.' Harriet stopped walking as she stepped on a stone in her bare feet.

He stopped immediately. 'All right?'

'Yes!' She stood on one leg and awkwardly tried to examine the sole of her other foot. 'Oh, it's nothing, I'll be fine.'

'Here.' And, before she knew what he was about, he'd picked her up and was carrying her towards the studio.

'You don't have to do this,' she protested after a silent, shocked couple of seconds.

'Too good an opportunity to allow to pass, on the other hand.'

'Mr Wyatt—'

'Ms Livingstone?' he parried. 'Surely we can go one step further—upstairs?' he asked as they arrived at the studio.

'Well, yes, but—'

'What I mean about one step further is surely we can use each other's given names now,' he said as he mounted the stairs and sat her down on the refectory table and examined the sole of her foot.

'Well, yes,' Harriet conceded and immediately felt like a broken record.

'Good. There's nothing wrong with your foot. You might have a bruise, that's all.'

'Thank you.' Harriet rested her palms on the table and could think of not another thing to say.

Damien Wyatt grimaced. 'OK,' he said. 'I seem to have rather bowled you over. Why don't we go our separate ways for the next couple of hours—I've got things to do anyway—then have dinner?'

Harriet licked her lips. 'I was planning to work.'

'Say that again.' Something rather chilly entered his eyes.

She blushed. 'I…' But she could only gesture helplessly.

'Still running away, Harriet?' he said softly.

'I…' She trailed off then gathered herself. 'There's nothing to run away from but—' she hesitated '—if you don't mind pasta you could come here for dinner.'

He looked surprised.

'What?' she queried.

'I guess I wasn't expecting that.'

'You may have some preconceived ideas about

me that influence your judgement; you obviously do,' she retorted.

There was a challenging glint in her eyes as she continued. 'Uh, let's see.' And she started to tick off her fingers. 'Head-in-the-clouds, accident-prone, academic—oh, let's not forget superior and neurotic. No wonder you were surprised to be asked to dinner!'

His lips twisted and he looked about to reply, then as if he'd changed his mind. He did say, 'I'll look forward to it. Around six? I'll bring some wine. You can stay,' he added to Tottie, who was looking visibly torn as he walked to the door.

Harriet stared at the doorway for a long moment after he'd disappeared then she clicked her fingers and Tottie came to the refectory table and put her chin on Harriet's knee with a soulful sigh.

'You could have gone with him,' she said as she stroked the dog's nose. 'I'd quite understand. He may not appreciate divided loyalties. In fact

I get the feeling he's a hard man with a lot of hang-ups.'

Tottie sat down and thumped her tail on the floor.

Harriet smiled then slid off the table and glanced at the kitchen clock and discovered she only had an hour to shower and change as well as produce dinner.

But when she reached the bathroom, she dropped the towel still wound round her and stared at herself in the mirror. Then she closed her eyes and breathed deeply as every sensation she'd experienced from the moment he'd picked her up in his arms and carried her upstairs to the moment he'd sat her down on the table—and beyond—came to her again.

The easy strength that had made her feel quite light despite her height. The movement of his muscles against her body, the feel of his heart beating against her as her own heartbeat had tripled. The hard wall of his chest that made her feel soft and so sensuous. The pure aroma of man she'd inhaled with delight…

She opened her eyes and stared at herself in something like shock as she thought—*this can't go on!*

It was a hurried shower she took. And she pulled on a pair of grey leggings patterned with white daisies and a white cotton shirt with puffed sleeves. She tied her hair back severely with a pink ribbon and didn't bother with any make-up, not that she needed any; walking in the sun and swimming in the sea the past few weeks had given her a golden glow.

'This is delicious but—correct me if I'm wrong—it's not pasta,' Damien said.

He'd changed into a denim shirt and jeans and they sat opposite each other at the refectory table that Harriet had set with blue woven mats, matching linen napkins and one of her herbs in a colourful pottery pot.

'Changed my mind,' she confessed. 'It's paella.'

'What's it got in it?'

Harriet rested her elbows on the table and dangled her fork in her fingers. 'Let's see, chicken and prawns, rice, saffron, of course, tomatoes, onions, garlic, baby peas—that's mainly it. I guess people have their own variations but that's mine.'

'If you'd told me I could have brought some Sangria.'

Harriet put her fork down and picked up her wine glass. 'It's a very nice Beaujolais.'

'Thanks. So,' he said thoughtfully, 'cooking is another of your accomplishments. You're a talented girl.'

'That's about the sum of it, though,' she said wryly. 'And I don't think I was born to cook. It came about through necessity.'

'How come?'

She explained about how she'd grown up.

'So that's why you're so protective of your brother,' he commented. 'I suppose in a way

I'm the same with Charlie. Our father died when he was seventeen. I've been standing in loco parentis ever since.' He grimaced.

Harriet pushed her plate away and picked up her glass. 'Charlie's a honey,' she said warmly.

Damien narrowed his eyes. 'He hasn't been chatting you up, has he?'

'Not at all. He's been trying to pin me down, if anything. As in trying to work me out. He believes, he says, anyway, I'm not like anyone else he's met. Mainly, from what I can gather—' she shrugged ruefully '—because of my work ethic.'

'How's it going, work-wise?'

Harriet studied her wine. 'Another week should do it.'

'You would have finished before I came home, if things had run to schedule, in other words.'

Harriet took a sip of her wine, put the glass down and plucked a basil leaf from the herb pot and crushed it between her fingers. 'Yes.'

He shrugged. 'Still hell-bent on being fancy-free, in other words?'

'Ah.' Harriet got up and collected their plates. She took them to the sink then opened the fridge and withdrew a lemon meringue dessert. She put it on the table, together with a tub of ice cream.

'If that's meant to placate me,' he said with a sudden wicked gleam of amusement in his dark eyes, 'you've hit the right button, ma'am. I cannot resist lemon meringue. Just don't tell the cook. He believes he and only he can make a perfect meringue. Incidentally, I'm in his black books.'

Harriet looked a question at him.

'He wanted to cook dinner for me.'

She smiled absently and set a coffee pot on to percolate. 'You're popular.'

He didn't respond and she sat down and served his dessert in silence.

'What about you? Of course,' he said, 'you don't have a sweet tooth.'

She nodded and he ate in silence until he said, 'You know, you haven't tripped or spilled anything tonight, which means you must be feeling more at ease so—can I put a proposition to you?'

Harriet blinked several times. 'What?'

'That we at least agree we have a rather devastating effect on each other.' He paused as Harriet looked away at the same time as she coloured.

'Yes,' she said after a long moment, and started as the coffee began to perk.

'I'll get it.' He got up and, without much fuss, found mugs and milk and sugar. 'However,' he continued, 'for reasons best known only to us, we're not keen to—start anything.' He looked briefly amused. 'Sounds a bit juvenile, doesn't it, but you probably get my drift.'

Harriet nodded.

'Incidentally, why did you,' he said as he began to pour the coffee, 'ask me to dinner tonight?'

Harriet hesitated. 'I...I felt I owed you some explanation.'

He sat down. 'You don't "owe" me anything,' he said abruptly.

'Mr...Damien,' Harriet said sternly, 'you told

me once you didn't appreciate being told what you should or should not feel, didn't you?'

He grimaced. 'Did I?'

'Yes! Well, I'm telling you I feel as if I owe you an explanation and that's that—damn!' she said with great feeling. 'Now you've got me all...' She trailed off frustratedly.

'Het up about nothing?' he suggested mildly.

She cast him a speaking look. 'Do you want to hear this or not?' she asked acerbically.

'Go ahead.'

'I fell in love. I...' She paused. 'I guess you could say I gave it my all. And we had...we did have some wonderful times. But then he noticed another woman and I could literally feel him slipping away from me. That's why...' She stopped.

'That's a fairly common thing to happen,' he said slowly. 'How long ago was this?'

'A year or so ago.' She shrugged.

'That's all?' he queried with a frown.

No, it's not all, Damien Wyatt, Harriet thought, but that's all you're getting, well...

'Well, I've wondered ever since whether I brought it on myself. I guess...' she twined her fingers together '...I may have been looking for someone to take over my life. No...' she frowned '...not that exactly, but someone I could depend on to make the right decisions for us. Rather than me having to, as I seemed to have grown up doing.

'But when it started to fall apart I couldn't help thinking I may have come across as too "needy" and it was probably a relief for him to get away,' she said with a wave of her hand. 'I still don't know the answer to that but, whatever, I'm not prepared to go through all that again. I thought...I should explain, though.' She hesitated because, of course, there was more but telling anyone was something she'd never been able to do yet...

Their gazes caught and held.

'But you don't seem to have that problem,' she

said at last. 'I mean I get the feeling you'd be quite happy to "start something".' Her glance was very blue and tinged with irony.

He crossed his arms and studied her thoughtfully. 'Yes, but, to be perfectly honest, if there is such a thing as...' he paused as if searching for the right phrase '...*love ever after*, I don't think it's going to exist for me.'

Harriet's eyes widened. 'Your marriage...' She trailed off awkwardly.

He raised an eyebrow at her. 'Isabel?'

'No. Charlie.'

He looked heavenward. 'I might have known.' Then, 'Well, you probably don't need me to elaborate.'

'All he told me was her name—and that he'd got firmly put in his place for merely mentioning it a little while back.'

Damien grimaced. 'Sounds like Charlie.'

'Sounds like you, actually.' A faint smile twisted her lips. 'So, it left you disillusioned?'

'It did a lot more damage.' He looked across

the room and his dark eyes were cold. 'But, yep, it certainly left me unwilling to repeat the experience—I know!' He raised his hand as Harriet opened her mouth. 'You're going to say with another woman it could be different. Perhaps. But not for me. I don't part easily from my grudges, be they personal or embracing an institution like marriage.'

Something like a shiver ran down Harriet's spine because she had a feeling his estimation of his character was correct…

'In a way, we're a bit alike,' he said then, drumming his fingers on the table. 'Too much responsibility at an early age, only it took us differently.' He paused, looking briefly humorous. 'You wanted someone to take over; I got too used to being in command to be able to bend at all.'

'How come?'

He shrugged. 'I was twenty-two when my father died. And we were about to be taken over so I had to stave that off and get us up and running again. That's when I made the dicey decision to expand into mining machinery when we'd always concentrated on agriculture and its machinery.

'Plus,' he said rather wryly, 'I think I was born with an "ornery" streak. Arthur agrees with me.'

'Talking of Arthur,' Harriet said with a smile, 'Penny is pregnant.'

Damien grimaced.

'You don't approve of her, do you?'

'I think she manipulates him shamelessly,' he said dryly, then grinned. 'He'll need plenty of support to get through this! He'll be a nervous wreck.'

Harriet laughed.

Damien put his coffee mug down and simply watched her. Her hair was tied back but becoming wayward as it escaped. Her skin was unbelievably smooth, her hands and wrists slender and elegant, and her eyes were like deep blue velvet and still sparkling with amusement.

He said slowly, with his dark gaze still resting

on her, 'I don't know how the hell I didn't see it the first time we met but you're breathtaking when you laugh.'

'I had nothing to laugh about at the time,' she said, still smiling. But gradually it faded as she moved awkwardly and nearly knocked her coffee over.

'So nothing's changed?' he said barely audibly as his gaze tracked her awkward movements.

'N-no,' she stammered.

'It doesn't make it easier that we've both stated our cases and I think we've both indicated we're not talking love ever after?'

Harriet tilted her head as she studied him with a frown in her eyes. 'No,' she said slowly.

'Any special reason?' he enquired dryly.

'I'm—I don't think I'm like that. I seem to be an all or nothing kind of person. In that regard,' she said thoughtfully.

Damien Wyatt smiled in a way that brought to mind an unamused tiger. 'You shouldn't go around saying things like that, Harriet Living-stone.'

'Why not? I think it's true.'

'It's also an incendiary kind of statement,' he murmured dryly.

Harriet looked at him wide-eyed. 'I…I'm not sure what you mean…' She faltered into silence. Then a flood of colour poured into her cheeks as his meaning became plain and she jumped up so precipitously she took Tottie by surprise and she tripped over her.

This time Damien Wyatt was too far away to rescue her and she'd fallen to her knees when he got to her.

'It's all right, I can manage,' she panted and held a hand out as if to ward him off as she scrambled to her feet. 'I didn't mean to…to imply,' she went on, 'what you obviously thought I meant to imply.'

'What was that?' he enquired and looked as if he was having trouble keeping his face straight as he steadied her with his hands on her waist.

'That—oh! You know what I mean!' Her expression was seriously frustrated.

'That you're only great in bed when you believe you're in love?'

She nodded then shook her head, more frustrated than ever. 'I didn't say anything about being great in bed and—'

'I'd like to bet you are, though,' he broke in.

'There's no way you could possibly know that!' she said heatedly.

He gestured. 'You're talking to a guy who's kissed you, remember?'

Harriet subsided a little. 'Well,' she said uncertainly.

'And you did suggest you were an *all or nothing* kind of person in *that* regard, which suggests—which conjures up certain images,' he said gravely, but she just knew his dark eyes were laughing at her.

She took a distressed breath and formed her hands into fists. 'Don't laugh at me,' she warned.

'Or?' he queried, his hands still on her waist.

'You don't expect to slug it out with me, do you?' He eyed her clenched fists.

'I would like nothing better,' she confirmed with great feeling again.

'How about testing out the other side of the coin?' he suggested, and pulled her closer.

She stiffened and urged herself into battle mode. Resist this, she told herself fiercely. Don't fall under his spell as you did last time, don't get mesmerised again. Don't allow the somehow simply wonderful feeling of being in his arms to overcome you and make you dizzy with delight. Dizzy and delighted because he feels so strong, because he knows just how and where to touch you and arouse you… She started as he spoke again.

'How about—this?' And he slid his fingers beneath her top and cupped her breasts.

CHAPTER FOUR

HARRIET TREMBLED AND he felt it through his fingers.

'If it's nice for you, you only need to nod,' he said huskily. 'Believe me—' he moved his fingers across her nipples '—it's sensational for me.'

Harriet's lips parted and she unclenched her fists and grasped his wrists instead. She didn't nod but she did say, 'You have a way of doing that—that's breathtaking but—'

'You'd rather I didn't?' he suggested, narrowing his eyes suddenly.

Harriet closed her eyes briefly. 'I'd much rather fly to the moon with you, Damien Wyatt,' she said barely audibly, 'but I can't help knowing I'd regret it sooner or later.'

'Another incendiary statement.'

She bit her lip. 'I'm sorry, I'm really sorry.' And there were tears in her eyes.

He hesitated for a long moment then he withdrew his hands and smoothed her top down. 'You win,' he drawled.

Harriet flicked away the tears on her cheeks and steeled herself for more mockery. It didn't come, not in the spoken form, anyway.

He turned away and sprawled out in one of the chairs at the table. 'Actually—' he ran a hand through his hair '—you're right, Ms Livingstone.'

But being right, Harriet discovered, didn't prevent him from subjecting her to a dark gaze full of dry amusement as he looked her up and down and mentally dispensed of all her clothes.

She bore that sardonic scrutiny and mental undressing for as long as she could, determined not to turn away and thereby give him the satisfaction of knowing he'd upset her, but was just about to protest when he spoke.

'Do you ride?'

Harriet blinked. 'Horses?'

'Well, I don't mean camels.'

'I have, as a kid,' she said cautiously.

He drummed his fingers on the table. 'Did you enjoy it?'

'Yes,' she replied but equally as cautiously as she wondered what was coming.

'Just tell me this, Harriet. Would it be purgatory for you if I suggested we get up at the crack of dawn tomorrow to take advantage of the low tide and go for a gallop down the beach? Tottie, I know, would love it.'

'If I could ride Sprite…' She paused and looked uncomfortable.

She saw him process this. 'So,' he murmured, 'you have a way with horses as well as dogs?'

Harriet spread her hands. 'Oh, I don't know.'

He raised an eyebrow. 'Sounds as if you've been chatting Sprite up already.'

'I suppose I have,' Harriet conceded ruefully.

'Then—are we on for tomorrow morning, about five?'

'I…' Harriet swallowed but nothing could stop the flow of images running through her mind of a dawn gallop followed by a swim then a huge breakfast. 'Yes,' she said.

'Good.' He stood up. 'Not—' he eyed her with a glint of pure devilry in his dark eyes '—that there'll be anything good about how to get to sleep tonight.'

It was no consolation to Harriet to reflect, as she tossed and turned in bed after Damien had gone, on one victory, one small victory perhaps, but all the same…

She'd successfully withstood the sensual on-slaught Damien could inflict on her, although *inflict* wasn't the right word for it at all. But she had withstood the power of his masculine ap-peal, she'd tacitly told him to do his worst when he'd mentally undressed her—and then she'd gone and wrecked it all by agreeing to go riding with him.

'Damn!' She sat up in bed. 'I must be mad. Apart from anything else, I know he's only going to lead me to fresh heartache—I should be running for my life!'

At five o'clock the next morning she felt heavy-eyed and in an uneven frame of mind as she pulled on jeans, a jumper and sand shoes.

Twenty minutes later, trotting down the track from the stables to the beach on the slightly fizzy Sprite, she was feeling marginally better, although only marginally, she assured herself.

By the time they reached the beach, the sun was turning the sky into a symphony of apricot as it hovered below the horizon and the placid waters reflected the colours back.

'Hang on,' Damien said as he took hold of Sprite's bridle and clipped on a leading rein so that she and Sprite were forced to adapt to his slower gait.

'What do you think you're doing?' Harriet asked.

'Taking precautions, that's all,' he replied.

'I can assure you, you don't need to!'

'You said you rode as a child. That could mean you haven't been on a horse for years.'

'I'm perfectly capable of riding this horse,' Harriet replied through her teeth.

'But you have to admit you're—well, if not exactly accident-prone, you do suffer from some weird syndrome that could cause all sorts of problems.'

'Mr Wyatt—' Harriet raised her riding crop '—don't say another word and let me go before I do something *you* might regret but *I* won't regret in the slightest!'

'Harriet,' he returned mildly, 'it's not very ladylike to keep attacking me.'

Harriet groaned. *'Let me go.'*

He hesitated briefly then unclipped the leading rein. Sprite, who'd been dancing around impatiently on the end of it, jostled his big brown horse, had the temerity to bestow a love bite on its neck, then, following Harriet's dictates, lengthened her stride and galloped away. Tottie raced after them joyously.

By the time they'd reached the end of the beach and galloped back, Harriet's mood had evened out—she was feeling far less grumpy and even of the opinion that this had been a good idea.

And, following Damien, she rode Sprite into the gentle low-tide surf. Both horses loved it and splashed energetically until finally they brought them out, led them to the edge of the beach and tied them loosely to trees.

'I'm soaked!' Harriet sank down onto the sand but she was glowing with enthusiasm as she sat cross-legged.

Damien cast himself down beside her and doodled in the sand with a twig. He hadn't shaved and he had a curious glint in his dark eyes as he looked across to study her.

'Tell me something,' he said. 'Are you not a morning person?'

Harriet opened her mouth, closed it, then she grinned. 'I am not. Well, not a very early morning person.' She was about to add—*and particularly not after a disturbed night*—but managed to hold that bit of information back. 'I take it you're the opposite?'

'Depends.'

'On what?'

'What's on offer in bed.'

Harriet looked heavenwards. 'Do men ever think of anything else?'

'Frequently.' He shot her an amused glance. 'Not, generally, at five in the morning with a warm, compliant partner, however.'

Harriet frowned as the wheels of her mind worked through this. Then she turned to him incredulously. 'Did you get me up at that ungodly hour as a shot at me for not...for...not... for being...for not being in bed with you?' she said exasperatedly.

'If I did,' he said wryly, 'I had no idea the danger I was placing myself in. I'll probably think twice before I do it again.'

'Oh!' Harriet ground her teeth as she stared at him, so big, so relaxed, so attractive, even if he hadn't shaved and his hair was hanging in his eyes, not to mention the fact that he was teasing her mercilessly.

'But of course,' he went on before Harriet could speak, 'the real reason I got you up at the crack of dawn was because of the tide. You need a low tide and therefore firm wet sand to gallop on. By the way, where did you learn to ride like that?'

Harriet closed her mouth and subsided somewhat. Then she shrugged and smiled. 'My father decided it needed to be part of my education. He restored a couple of valuable paintings for a wealthy horse breeder who was once a jockey in exchange for riding lessons. He had a few other notions along those lines—I had tennis lessons under similar circumstances, not so successful; my—' she cast him a quirky glance '—weird syndrome interfered with me becoming a Wimbledon champion.'

He laughed and looked at her curiously again. 'You're full of surprises—docile and ladylike on one hand then quite a termagant.'

'Docile!' Harriet pulled a face. 'That sounds awful. So does termagant. I'm sure I'm not either of those.'

'You're also younger sometimes. The ladylike you could be ten years older.'

'That's ridiculous,' Harriet objected but found she had to laugh a little. 'You know, the art world takes itself very seriously sometimes, so one may get into the habit of *being* very serious-minded without quite realising it.'

He laughed then glanced at his watch. 'OK. I've got things to do.'

He got up and untied his horse but Harriet stayed where she was, quite unaware that she looked disappointed.

'Harriet?'

She looked up to see him frowning down at her.

'This is how you want it, isn't it?' he queried.

She froze then a heartbeat later she scrambled up. 'Sure! Let's go!'

But upstairs in the flat after she'd showered and was eating breakfast alone, it wasn't how she wanted it at all, she had to confess to herself.

She worked furiously for the next couple of days then Charlie came home for a long weekend and it was his birthday and he'd decided to have a party.

If she hadn't been so engrossed in her work, she'd have noticed the preparations going on in the big house, but she hadn't. Therefore it took her by surprise when Isabel asked her what she'd be wearing.

'Wearing?'

'To Charlie's birthday party.'

'When?'

Isabel clicked her tongue. 'Tomorrow. You're invited.'

'No I'm not.' Harriet put down the ivory figu-rine of a dolphin she was holding.

'But I put an invitation—' Isabel broke off, looked around and stepped over to the table be-side the door where she picked up several items of mail, one of which she then brandished at Harriet, looking exasperated. 'Even if you didn't see this, surely you noticed that something was going on?'

Harriet coloured. 'No. I'm sorry. And thank you very much for inviting me—'

'Charlie did,' Isabel corrected.

'Charlie then, but I couldn't possibly come.'

'Why on earth not?' Isabel stared at her with the light of battle clearly lit in her dark Wyatt eyes.

Harriet heaved a sigh. 'I'm—I'm an employee, Isabel,' she said but tartly despite the sigh, 'and don't forget it! Look, I'm sorry if I sound snippy or rude but sometimes it's the only way to deal with you Wyatts.' To her horror, tears stood out in her eyes but she carried on relentlessly. 'I'm not coming and that's that.'

'Not coming where?'

Both Harriet and Isabel swung around to see Damien standing in the doorway.

'Charlie's party,' Isabel said bitterly.

Harriet turned away. There had been no more dawn rides on the beach; in fact she'd hardly seen Damien since that magical morning.

'That's OK,' Damien said easily. 'It's her choice.'

Isabel took a sharp angry breath. 'Men! You're all the same; never there for you when you're needed. If anyone could have persuaded her, you could have. But, on top of being unreliable, most men are as thick as planks!' And she stormed past Damien and out into the night.

Harriet closed her mouth and blinked several times.

'Ditto,' Damien murmured. 'You wouldn't change your mind and come, would you, Harriet? If for no other reason than for me to regain some credibility in my aunt's eyes.'

Harriet hesitated then sighed. 'I might just put in an appearance. But that's all,' she warned.

'Far be it from me to urge you otherwise,' he said gravely. 'No, I wouldn't dream of persuading you to take part in what you might see as mindless revelry in some way beneath you—or whatever. So, goodnight, Miss Livingstone,' he added reverently and he too stepped out into the night. He also closed the door.

Harriet discovered herself to be possessed of a burst of anger and she picked up an object to hurl it at the door, only to realise it was the ivory dolphin.

She lowered it to the table, breathing heavily, and she said to Tottie, 'That was a close call.'

Tottie wagged her tail and went back to sleep.

By eight o'clock the next evening, Charlie's party was starting to hum. The lounge had been cleared for dancing, a disco had been set up and the dining room hosted a magnificent buffet and a bar.

Guests from all over the Northern Rivers had descended on Heathcote, some from further afield like the Gold Coast.

Harriet got to know this because Charlie personally came to escort her to the party.

She looked down at herself just before Charlie climbed the stairs to the flat—not that she'd known he was coming. In fact she was grappling with nerves and the desire to find a hole to fall into. She was also hoping she wasn't over- or underdressed.

She wore a black dress with a loose skirt to just above her knees with white elbow-length sleeves and white panels in the bodice. It was a dress that emphasised the slenderness of her waist. With it she had on a ruby-red chunky necklace, her legs were golden and long and bare and she wore black suede high heels with ankle ties.

Her hair was pulled back into a knot but she'd

coaxed some tendrils to frame her face. Her lips were painted a delicious shimmering pink and her eyes were made up with smoky shadow, her lashes just touched with mascara to emphasise their length.

'Holy Mackerel!'

Charlie stopped dead as he stepped into the flat and took in every detail about Harriet.

'Oh, boy!' he said then.

Harriet twisted her hands together. 'What's wrong?'

'It's not that, it's the opposite. Poor old Damien; is he in for…well. I hope you know what you're doing, Harriet.'

'Doing?'

Charlie blinked and frowned. 'You didn't set out to drive him wild?' He gestured to take her in from the tip of her head to her toes.

Harriet opened her mouth to deny this accusation but she closed it and coloured slightly. 'I haven't actually worn it before. Is it too…?' She didn't complete the sentence. 'I can change.'

'Don't you dare!' Charlie looked horrified. 'So you did set out to drive him wild?'

'I did not,' she denied.

'I wouldn't mind,' Charlie offered. 'I'm on your side.'

'I…' Harriet hesitated. 'He made a remark that cast me in the light of a docile priggish bore. So I thought I'd show him otherwise. But now, if you must know, Charlie, I'm sorry, but I really don't want to go to your party.'

'Made a remark, did he?' Charlie ignored the rest of her statement. 'He's done that to me. He has a way of doing it that makes you want to throw things—but what sweet revenge would this be. Come, my lady Harriet.' He held out his arm.

'Charlie…Charlie, this is not really me and I've changed my mind about…showing him anything.'

'No, you haven't,' Charlie disagreed as he led her to the top of the stairs. 'You've got a slight case of stage fright, that's all. But I'll be there!'

* * *

'So.'

Harriet stood on the terrace, sipping champagne and fanning herself.

There was a moon. There were also flaming braziers in the garden and the music flowing out was of a solid rock beat and loud enough to drown the sound of the surf beyond the garden wall.

'So,' she repeated without turning.

'You don't mind a dance, Miss Livingstone,' Damien observed, moving forward to stand beside her.

'I don't. At the right time and place,' she replied. She took another sip of champagne as she registered the fact that he was wearing a tweed jacket over a round-necked shirt, and jeans.

'I thought you were just going to put in an appearance.'

'I was. Your brother had other ideas.' She shrugged.

'You look—great. Quite unlike your alter ego.'

'Thank you. I suppose you mean my academic, neurotic—' she waved a hand '—and all the rest of it, side.'

'Well, certainly the you that looks as if you've stepped straight out of Christies or Sotheby's or a museum.' He paused then glanced across at her. 'What would happen if I asked you to dance?'

'Thank you so much, Damien, but—' she drained her champagne and put the glass down on the table beside her '—I think I've done enough partying,' she finished politely.

Their gazes locked. 'That's a pity.' He raised a dark eyebrow. 'Still scared and running, Harriet?'

Harriet put a hand to her throat. 'We've been through all this, Damien.'

He shrugged and studied his beer tankard. 'I don't think we made allowances for the effects of you looking so gorgeous and seriously sexy, you dancing, your legs on show; no sign of the eternal jeans or leggings you wear. It's almost as if you're issuing an invitation, Miss Livingstone.'

A tide of colour poured into Harriet's cheeks.

He studied it with interest. 'You are?'

'No. Oh! Look,' she said intensely, 'you persuaded me to come to this party. You then made—talk about an incendiary remark but in quite a different sense—you made my blood boil *in anger*,' she emphasised, 'with your comments about mindless revelry that I would find beneath me.'

'So you decided to show me a thing or two?' he hazarded.

'Yes,' she said through her teeth. 'Mind you—' she hesitated then decided she might as well go for broke '—I did intend only to put in an appearance, enjoy myself for a little while then retreat. The music got to me,' she added.

His lips twitched. 'I quite understand. The music is getting to me right now, as a matter of fact.'

Harriet narrowed her eyes and concentrated

for a moment as she listened to the music, and grimaced.

'No good for you?' he queried as she barely restrained herself from moving to the beat.

'I couldn't exactly say that...'

'We could have a "no hands" agreement,' he suggested. 'We could just do our own thing,' he explained.

Harriet eyed him. 'What a good idea.' She smiled sweetly then laughed at his expression. 'It's OK. I'll take my chances.'

It was a phrase that was to haunt her during the rest of that night and the day that followed.

Because the fact of the matter was, she'd danced the rest of the night away with Damien.

She'd rocked and rolled, she'd been quiet and peaceful in his arms. She'd revelled in the feel of his hands on her, in the feel of his body against hers. She'd followed his lead and adapted her steps to his, once with a flourish that had flared her skirt out around her thighs so that she'd grimaced and pushed it down with a tinge of colour in her cheeks.

As she'd danced she'd recalled the last time she'd been in his arms and the intimacy of the way they'd kissed. And she'd wished they were alone as they'd been that day so she could run her fingers through the thick darkness of his hair and slide her hands beneath his jacket and shirt and feel those sleek muscles of his back…

And at the end she'd been wrapped in his arms, barely moving and loving it.

That was when the lights had come on. That was when people had started to leave. That was when she'd come to her senses, when she'd looked up into his eyes, when she'd seen the desire in them.

And when she'd freed herself urgently and fled from him, melting into the crowd of departing guests then running up the stairs to the flat, locking herself in and turning off all the lights.

She'd undressed shakily and thrown her dress onto the floor.

But as she'd climbed under the doona she'd known it was futile and ridiculous to blame a dress. She was the one to blame. She was the one who'd been unable to resist the feel of his arms around her, the one who'd got an incredible rush from matching her body to his as they'd danced. The one who had lost all her inhibitions at the hands of Damien Wyatt when she'd promised herself it was the last thing she would do…

There was no sign of Damien the next day.

In fact it was a curiously quiet day. Once the after-party clean-up had taken place, it was as if all the Wyatts and everyone else had melted away.

Isabel, at least, had explained that she was going to spend the night with a friend.

Charlie, Harriet assumed, had gone back to his base.

Not that she particularly wanted to face anyone after last night but it somehow added to her mood of doom and gloom to find herself feeling as if she were alone on the planet.

She'd just eaten her dinner when she heard footsteps on the outside stairway, and Damien arrived.

She half got up, sat down again and trembled inwardly at his expression.

Tottie was, of course, delighted to see him.

Harriet stood up again and collected her plate and knife and fork. 'I'm sorry,' she said. 'I don't know what got into me last night.'

'I didn't come to conduct a post-mortem into last night.' He looked at her sardonically. 'Any idea where Isabel is? She usually leaves a note.'

Harriet explained about the friend.

He looked even more irritated. 'Did she say which fr—?'

He stopped abruptly as Tottie growled suddenly and then, in a manner of speaking, all hell broke loose.

There was a whoosh of sound and the sky beyond the windows of the flat illuminated briefly in the direction of the house.

'What the devil...?' Damien shut his teeth hard then went on, 'It's the kitchen. Looks like the cook has finally decided to burn the place down.'

The cook hadn't—at least not consciously had he decided to burn the place down—but he had got drunk and he had allowed oil in a deep fryer to catch alight as he'd dozed with a bottle of bourbon in his fist.

He still had it—the bourbon bottle in his fist— when Harriet and Damien arrived on the scene as he stared, stupefied, from the relative safety of the vegetable garden, at the flames leaping out of the kitchen windows.

But within moments, or so it seemed, Damien had taken control. He'd rung for the fire brigade, he'd sent Harriet to waken Stan, the stable foreman, who was the only other person on the property, and he'd located several fire extinguishers, hoses and fire blankets. He also took a moment to attempt to send Harriet back up-stairs to the flat.

'No,' she shouted over the crackling of the flames, 'I can hold a hose!'

'Yeah, but I don't want you tripping and fall-ing over!'

'Listen to me, Damien Wyatt,' she yelled at him, 'it's only you who makes me do that—look out,' she screamed as a burning piece of wood fell from a window ledge right next to him.

He leapt away and she grabbed a hose and sprayed the sparks that had fallen on his boots and jeans.

'All right, listen,' he said. 'Be careful; be very careful.'

'I will, I will,' she promised fervently.

He stared down at her in the demonic fire-light, then hugged her to him, and immediately turned away.

It was a frenetic scene as they tried to tame the leaping, crackling flames glowing orange against the background of a midnight-blue sky, a scene also of choking smoke pouring from the kitchen and a stifling charred smell.

And by the time the fire brigade arrived Harriet was blackened and soaked to the skin.

'Don't.' Damien loomed up in front of her and removed her hose from her hand. 'Don't do any more; you've done enough. It's under control now.'

'But…'

'Just do as I tell you, Harriet Livingstone,' he said and, without further ado, kissed her full on the lips. 'Be a good girl and go and get cleaned up.'

CHAPTER FIVE

HARRIET WENT, WITH the tips of her fingers pressed to her lips.

And she grimaced at the sight of herself as she went to take her third shower of the day. She dressed in jeans and a track top and concentrated on clearing away her dinner and putting a fresh pot of coffee on to perk.

Sounds of all the activity were starting to scale down as she worked, and finally she heard the fire engine drive away and an almost unnatural silence overtake Heathcote.

Not much later Damien and Tottie turned up, Damien also showered and in clean clothes, a grey track top and khaki cargo pants, and bearing a bottle of brandy.

Harriet reached for glasses. 'You must be a mind-reader.'

He grimaced. 'Nothing like a good fire to provoke the need for some Dutch courage.' He splashed two generous tots into the glasses.

'How bad is it?'

'The kitchen—cheers,' he said and touched his glass to hers, 'the kitchen will have to be rebuilt. Thankfully, it didn't go any further.'

'How's the cook?'

Damien shook his head. 'A sodden wreck. Stan's looking after him. He's full of remorse and petrified he's going to lose his job.'

Harriet paused with her glass halfway to her mouth. 'He expects to keep it after nearly burning the place down?'

Damien shrugged and his lips twisted. 'According to Isabel, he's got six kids stashed away in Queensland so I'll get her to find him a position closer to home.'

Harriet looked surprised.

He looked wry. 'You didn't expect that?'

'Well, no,' she said. 'Sorry.'

'That's OK. I'm used to being in your bad books or, if not that, then suspected of some kind of dodginess or another.' He drained some of his brandy. 'Incidentally, we're going to have to use this kitchen until we get the house kitchen fixed.' He looked around.

'Oh. Of course.' She got up and poured the coffee and brought it back to the table. 'I don't suspect you of *dodginess*, whatever that means precisely.' She pushed his mug over to him and sat down with hers.

He drank some more brandy. 'You obviously suspect me of something, Miss Livingstone.'

Harriet grimaced. 'I did tell Isabel I thought you were a bit of a control freak.'

'What brought that on?'

Harriet looked at him askance. 'The car you insisted I drive.'

'Oh, that.' He lounged back and shoved his hands into his pockets.

Harriet studied him. His dark hair was still

damp and there were blue shadows on his jaw. He looked perfectly relaxed and not as if he'd just fought a fire. For some reason, to have him so big and powerful and quite at ease in what she'd come to regard as her home annoyed her. 'Yes, that,' she said tartly.

He lifted his shoulders. 'I wouldn't be so far off the mark in believing you and your brother's vehicle were something of a menace on the roads but—' he sat up '—before you take umbrage, just the sight of it annoyed me enormously.'

Harriet stared at him.

'Does it make me a control freak to provide you with an alternative, though?' he mused gently. 'I don't believe so.'

Harriet continued to stare at him as several things ran through her mind. She'd experienced a maelstrom of emotions due solely to this man. She'd never stopped thinking about Damien Wyatt while he'd been away, even if she had been able to bury it in her subconscious. She'd been physically stirred by him. She'd told him some of her painful history. She'd cooked him dinner—she'd even made him a lemon meringue dessert.

She'd danced with him, ridden with him, been hugged and kissed by him—she could still feel the imprint of his mouth on hers, come to think of it—and her fingers went to her lips involuntarily at the mere thought of it.

Only to see that he was watching her intently.

She snatched her hand away as a tide of pink rose in her cheeks, then threw up her hands in serious frustration. 'Look,' she said levelly, 'because I'm not prepared to jump into bed with you doesn't mean to say I think you're dodgy, although it's just as bad but quite the opposite really.'

He frowned. 'What does that mean?'

Harriet bit her lip and could have shot herself—if ever she'd voiced an unwise utterance this was it…

'It doesn't matter,' she said stiffly.

'Oh, come on, Harriet,' he said impatiently, 'I

can take it.' He looked briefly amused. 'Spit it out, Miss Livingstone.'

Harriet glared at him. 'If you must know, I suspect you of being far too good in bed, Mr Wyatt, for any girl's peace of mind.'

He sobered completely and stared at her narrowly. 'How, one has to ask,' he said slowly, 'did you work that out?'

Her eyes were full of irony. 'You're talking to a girl who's kissed you, remember?'

His lips twisted. 'So you did. Well—' he drained his glass and stood up '—on that note I think I'll leave you to your memories, Miss Livingstone, and I will take mine…somewhere else. Goodnight.' And he patted her on the head, told Tottie to stay put, and strolled out.

Harriet stared after him in a state of suspended animation. In other words, with her mouth open and her eyes huge and dark with disbelief.

Was this his retaliation for what she'd done last night?

Why did she feel disbelief, though? she found

herself wondering. Because she'd been convinced he would react differently to what had
been—talk about incendiary!—another incendiary statement she'd made.

All the same, a true statement, she reasoned
with herself. She *was* deadly afraid that once
she gave in to Damien Wyatt she'd be hooked.
She'd be on a roundabout, in love with a man
who didn't believe in love, who didn't believe
in marriage…

As if she hadn't had enough trauma in that
direction.

Damien Wyatt, after checking his property over
thoroughly, and making sure the cook was in
no position to do any more damage, climbed
the stairs and walked into his bedroom but he
didn't immediately go to bed. He didn't even
turn the light on.

He stood instead at the open window and listened to the sea crashing onto the beach. From
the sound of it, he judged it to be high tide or

close to it. And he could see a tracing of phosphorous lying luminous on the beach as each wave receded.

But he was only registering the phosphorous absently. He was thinking of Harriet Livingstone. He could see her in his mind's eye, serving up her paella and her lemon meringue with that slim tall figure in daisy-patterned leggings and a white blouse.

Thinking of her last night as she'd looked lovely enough to stir any man's blood. And had danced in her own way, a way that was enough to tempt any man.

And tonight, soaked to the skin and her hands and face blackened, then clean and neat again in jeans and a track top.

Hearing her saying the kind of things women who were not naïve couldn't say with a straight face—she was an all or nothing person in that direction. Sex and relationships, in other words. Accusing him of being too good in bed for her peace of mind…

He fingered the curtain then turned away and threw himself down in an armchair. The room was still in darkness but there was a lamp on the table beside the armchair. He pressed the button and soft light radiated from under the silk shade. And the bedroom came alive in its blue and gold trappings.

He'd inherited the master bedroom when his parents had passed away, although he hadn't moved into it until he'd married, and it still reflected his mother's taste. A four-poster bed, flocked wallpaper, tapestries—if it wasn't a superbly comfortable bed he'd have left the grandeur of this bedroom, which made him think it should belong in a French chateau, to darkness and silence after he and Veronica had separated.

Or, he mused, maybe it wasn't only the bed. Perhaps he continued to use the room as a warning to himself never to forget the trauma and betrayal Veronica had brought to him.

Maybe…

But where to place Harriet Livingstone in his scheme of things?

He moved restlessly. It was unfortunate but true, he had to admit, that he was extremely attracted to her, even if he couldn't quite analyse why.

What was more unfortunate about it was that he believed her when she said she wasn't built for affairs. Why he believed her, he couldn't say. Why he didn't see it as a ploy on her behalf to tell him she was an all or nothing girl, a ploy to set him on fire physically in a manner of speaking, he couldn't say either.

But what he'd considered the natural progression from a spontaneous attraction that had gripped them *both* was now fraught with all sorts of dangers…

It always had been from her point of view, he found himself conceding. She'd always known it was a road she couldn't, or shouldn't, travel.

He'd always thought, he conceded too with an inward grimace, that he could break her down or win her over to something that was fulfill-ing, pleasant but not too deep—no, not too deep.

'You're a fool, Damien Wyatt,' he told him-self. 'Too blind to see that she is that kind of girl—a genuinely all or nothing girl. A girl who could be devastated if you had a relationship but didn't marry her—and now you've got to with-draw somehow.

'Why would it be so impossible to marry her?'

A pool of silence swallowed up his question.

Because he didn't believe he could trust any woman again? And therefore he didn't want to inflict the worst of his cynicism on Harriet Liv-ingstone?

He stood up abruptly. The sooner he distanced himself from her the better.

Harriet, to her surprise, fell asleep as soon as her head touched the pillow and she slept deeply and dreamlessly the night of the fire.

As she studied herself in the bathroom mir-ror the next morning she couldn't help but notice that, despite that night of quality sleep, she looked tense. There seemed to be an undertone of worry to her expression.

'Damien,' she said softly to herself. 'Things between us are—a worry, aren't they? What am I going to do?'

She left the bathroom and suddenly remembered her kitchen would be on call and the least she could do was have some coffee ready.

It was Isabel who arrived first, looking shocked.

'Damien rang me earlier,' she told Harriet, puffing a bit after climbing the stairs. 'Thank heavens it didn't spread. I should have done something about Cook before now,' she added with a sigh. 'Thanks for helping to put it out.'

'I didn't do much, other than pointing a hose. Would you like some coffee?'

'Love some. I'm afraid you're stuck with me for meals and I'm not much of a cook,' Isabel confessed.

'That's OK. I enjoy it. In fact I was just going to cook some bacon and eggs for breakfast.'

'Yum! I'll stay put then.'

'What about Damien?' Harriet asked as she reached into the fridge for her breakfast ingredients.

'Oh, he's gone off again. Perth this time. Not sure when he'll be back. He's got some South African mining magnate he's dealing with.' Isabel waved a hand.

'Oh,' Harriet said.

'Didn't he mention it? I suppose he didn't have time,' Isabel continued without waiting for a response. 'He's left me screeds of instructions to do with the kitchen—you know, it did need renovating and modernising.' Isabel chuckled.

Harriet smiled as well, but it wasn't really an amused smile.

'So.'

It was late in the afternoon and she was sitting on a bench with Tottie beside her on a small headland just south of Heathcote homestead. It was an overcast day with a cool breeze that was lifting Tottie's shaggy coat and causing the seagulls to plane on the thermals.

They'd been for a long brisk walk and were on their way home now.

'So,' Harriet said again. 'It's all off, Tottie. Your master has walked away without a word and I should be celebrating because I've always—almost—known I was playing with fire just by being anywhere near him.'

'I'm not—' she put her arm around Tottie '—celebrating, though. I'm miserable. I feel abandoned. I feel hard done by because he can come and go while I'm stuck here because of his mother's collection, because of Brett, not that I hold Brett responsible for anything...'

She stared out over the silvery sea. It was a choppy seascape today with whitecaps that, if you knew anything about matters maritime, told you the breeze was running at about twenty knots.

How did I know that? she wondered. Must have been amongst quite a lot of the useless information I learnt from Dad. Is any information useless, though?

She continued to stare out to sea and grimaced as she saw a yacht sailing south and riding the waves a bit like a rocking horse. Then she felt Tottie stiffen and saw her nose quiver as she tested the wind. The final giveaway as the big dog bounded to her feet was the joyful bark she reserved for one person and one person only—Damien.

Harriet scrambled to her feet and there he was, climbing the headland towards them. Then she stood like a statue until he was right up to them and her eyes were wide and astonished because he wore a suit and a tie.

'I thought…I thought you were in Perth,' she stammered.

'I had planned to be,' he replied as he made a fuss of Tottie, 'but something wouldn't let me go.'

'What?' she asked huskily, her expression mystified.

'You.'

She blinked several times. 'I don't understand.'

'You once believed you owed me an explanation. I've come under the same compulsion.'

He paused and loosened his tie and once again the way the breeze lifted his dark hair gave her goose bumps.

'I thought it was best for us to—just cut this thing between us,' he said then, his dark eyes resting on the riot of curls in her hair the wind had whipped up. 'I thought that last night and right until I got to Sydney airport from Ballina this morning,' he said dryly. 'Then I changed my mind and flew back. Or, rather, it got changed for me by some arcane process I don't quite understand, but anyway—'

He stopped and looked around. 'Do you want to hear this here or back down—?'

'Here,' she broke in.

So they sat down on the bench and Tottie

lay down at their feet with a look of pure contentment.

'It's about Veronica,' he said. 'She was, as Charlie insisted on putting it—' he looked heavenwards '—just gorgeous. Not only that; she was bright. She ran her own IT consultancy business. We had an affair, then we got married.

'I have to say,' he went on thoughtfully, 'that we fought as spectacularly as we did the opposite. But she wasn't cut out to stay at home and run things like Isabel does. That was something I often found irritating and often—' he shrugged '—held against her. Mind you, she had her own list of sins she held against me and, to be honest, the relationship was foundering. Then she discovered she was pregnant and, although she'd been rather secretive about it, I thought— it seemed to be a calming influence. I didn't realise she was simply subdued and—worried.'

Harriet looked down at her hands.

'And the baby came, a boy, no problems, until he was about six months old. Then he was diagnosed with a blood disorder and both Veronica and I were tested to establish our blood groups et cetera. That's when it emerged—' Damien stared out to sea for a long moment '—that I wasn't the baby's father.'

Harriet gasped.

'As you say,' he commented with some irony. 'At least that was my first reaction. Of course, after that, things got...much more animated. Accusations running thick and fast, along the lines of *Had she always been unfaithful?* Coming from me, that one,' he said. 'To be answered along the lines of *Who wouldn't be unfaithful to someone as cold and bloody-minded as me?* Hang on.'

He retrieved his mobile from his pocket, glanced at it and switched it off.

'So, as you can imagine, it was a shambles.'

'Yes,' Harriet breathed.

'It became even more so,' he said after a time.

'How?'

'It turned out she couldn't be sure *who* the father was but she'd reasoned I was the best bet, financially, anyway.'

Harriet put her hands to her face. 'She was… was she…?'

'She was promiscuous,' he said. 'That's probably a polite way of putting it. Of course I'd known I wasn't the first but it might be hard for you to imagine what it feels like to know you've been in a line of men even after the wedding, not to mention having some other man's child palmed off on you.'

'I'm surprised she kept the baby.'

'So was I,' he agreed, 'but I think she saw it as some kind of a hold over me if things got really tough between us. In the normal course of events, we may never have discovered he wasn't mine.'

'What happened to him?'

Damien stared out to sea. 'I made Veronica find out who the father was and these days, with DNA testing—' he shrugged '—you can do it and there's no way it can be denied. So I divorced her.' He stopped rather abruptly.

'Did you…did you have any kind of affection for the baby, when you thought he was yours?'

He frowned. 'I don't know if I had some premonition but no, not a lot. But I don't know if it was simply that I'm just not good with babies. Actually, I felt more for the poor kid when I found out he wasn't mine. And I've set up a trust for him and made sure that at least he'll know who his father is. I also paid for the procedures and treatment he needed and of course Veronica got a generous settlement. End of story.'

He got up and walked to the edge of the headland, staring out to sea with his hands pushed into his pockets and the breeze blowing his tie around.

'Of course not the end of the story,' he said over his shoulder and came back to sit down beside her.

'I didn't think it was,' Harriet said quietly, 'but—'

'Look,' he interrupted, 'if you're going to tell me it's highly unlikely it could ever happen for me like that again, you're right. The odds against it are enormous. I *know* that—intellectually. That doesn't mean to say I can make myself believe it in my heart. That doesn't mean to say I can bury all my cynicism, all my—' he broke off and shrugged '—disbelief that I could have been taken for such a flat.'

'Did you never suspect?' Harriet asked curiously.

'Sometimes. But she was good at diverting any doubts I may have had. And I'm not trying to say I was blameless myself. If anything was going to work for Veronica in a marriage, it was an anchorman. I could work that out, I could see,' he said intensely, 'that she was one of those high-powered people who often didn't know how to come down from the heights. But I couldn't…I—' he closed his eyes briefly '—just got more and more irritated and difficult to live with.'

Harriet looked across at him. His profile was rock-hard and she could see the tension in the set of his mouth and his shoulders. 'How can you be *sure* you're going to feel like this with another woman?'

'I've had a couple of—' he shrugged '—liaisons since then. They didn't last. I didn't want them to last because I felt stifled,' he said. 'I wanted to be free. I never, ever want to go through that kind of trauma again.'

He paused then he said sardonically, 'I would never have thought I was naïve going into marriage with Veronica; I certainly wasn't afterwards. I kept looking for signs, pointers, indicators that I was being taken for a fool again so that those liaisons became a nightmare of mistrust.'

He broke off and sighed. 'And I keep thinking of the consequences and how one innocent child got caught up in it all. That's why I'm better on my own. But I had to tell you this. Despite the fact that this attraction lies between us, it could never be more than that.'

He put his hand over hers. 'I'm sorry.'

Harriet blinked away a tear. 'That's OK.'

He paused then looked at her curiously. 'You really don't mind?'

Harriet smiled, just a gentle curve of her mouth. 'Yes, I do mind a bit but I always knew it couldn't work for me, so—'

'You're still in love with—whoever he was?'

Harriet considered and realised that until quite recently she might have believed that. Not any more, however. But it made no difference now. There was no future for her with Damien Wyatt…

She blinked several times as it hit her like a train all of a sudden that it mattered greatly to her to think there was no future for her with this man. He couldn't have spelled it out more clearly.

So, she thought, the tables have turned. I was

the one who was eager to cut 'things' off between us; now I'm the one who…'

'Harriet?'

'Uh—I don't know. But, for my own reasons, I
really don't want to get involved like that again.
You probably think I'm silly.' She stopped and
shrugged.

There was a long silence. Then he said, 'Tottie will be devastated.'

Harriet smiled and blew her nose. 'Well, I
ought to get back to work. Do you—' she hesitated '—do you want me to finish your mother's things?'

'Yes,' he replied promptly. 'I won't be here—
no, I'm not going to try to go to Perth again
today, but tomorrow I will.'

'Oh.' Harriet jumped up with a hand to her
mouth. 'I'm cook tonight. I promised Isabel
roast beef. Will you…?' She looked a question
at him.

'Roast beef,' he repeated, his dark eyes full of
amusement. 'Something else I can't resist.'

* * *

Harriet's roast beef was rare on the inside and dark brown on the outside. With it she served roast potatoes and pumpkin, green beans and a rich gravy.

'Mmm, that was delicious,' Isabel enthused as she put her knife and fork together. 'A girl of many talents!'

'She is,' Damien agreed and raised his glass to Harriet. 'If ever you need a job away from the job you do, you know where to come.'

'Apart from anything else, we know you won't burn down the kitchen,' Isabel said mischievously.

'On that subject, how is the gentleman—where is he?' Damien asked.

'I packed him off home to his wife and family today with three months' pay and a couple of contacts, both restaurants where he'd be too busy to get drunk and lonely. That wouldn't be sticky date pudding, by any chance?' Isabel asked of

Harriet with equal proportions of trepidation and longing in her voice.

It was and it not only found favour with Isabel but also her nephew.

'Amazing.' he said, 'For someone who hasn't got a sweet tooth to produce such amazing desserts is quite—amazing.'

They all laughed.

'So you'll be in South Africa? For how long?' Isabel queried of Damien. 'Incidentally—' she frowned '—why did you come back today?'

'Something came up,' Damien replied. 'And I don't know how long I'll be in South Africa—a few weeks at least. As to why I'm going, there's a lot of mining in Africa.'

Isabel stood up and insisted on clearing the table and loading the dishwasher but she declined coffee and, with a yawn and her thanks for a perfect meal, she left them alone.

'You know—' Damien swirled the last of his Merlot in his glass '—I've been thinking. Why don't you stay on when all my mother's stuff is sorted? That's going to happen much sooner than your brother walking again by the sound of it. How is he doing?'

Harriet told him. 'He's got a new physio, a woman. I think he's fallen in love with her. Not too seriously, I hope.'

Damien grimaced. 'She's probably used to it and knows how to handle it. But if it's contributing towards his progress, it might be worth a few heartaches for him. Or...' he stretched his legs out '...who knows, it might become mutual. Anyway, to get back to this place, why don't you stay on? Isabel really enjoys your company. And I'm sure Charlie does too, when he's home.'

'I won't have anything to do, though,' Harriet objected.

Damien sat up. 'I've been thinking about that. Periodically, Arthur sends our paintings away to be cleaned. It's about that time now, so why don't *you* do it? Here.'

Harriet's eyes widened and her mouth fell open.

'Isn't that what your father did?'

Her jaw clicked as she closed her mouth. 'Yes. Well, he restored paintings too.' She stopped abruptly and bit her lip.

'Then?'

'I couldn't.' She clasped her hands on the table. 'I'd feel like a charitable institution.'

'Nonsense.' His tone was biting. 'It's a good business proposition. Arthur agrees.'

Harriet frowned. 'When have you had time to consult Arthur?'

'In this day and age of mobile phones it only took a few minutes. Did you think I had to rely on carrier pigeons or the bush telegraph?'

Harriet compressed her lips and looked at him mutinously.

'For crying out loud, just say yes, Harriet Livingstone.' He shoved his hand through his hair wearily. 'Thanks to you, I've been up since the crack of dawn, I've had to fly to Sydney and back again, not to mention loitering around Sydney Airport waiting for bloody flights.'

'I didn't ask you to do any of that!' she protested.

'Nevertheless, it was all due to you. Look, I won't be here, if that's what's worrying you. No coming home early this time.' He gazed at her ironically.

'But it could take me…a month!' She tried to visualise every painting in the house. 'It's very painstaking, careful work done properly.'

He pushed his wine glass away. 'I'll go on a safari,' he said flippantly. 'There's a lot of wildlife in Africa as well as mining.'

Harriet got up and put her hands on her hips. 'You're impossible.'

'That's what my wife used to tell me,' he drawled.

Harriet flinched then shrugged. 'She may have been right.'

'No doubt.' He watched her as she paced around the table. She'd changed into white pedal pushers and a loose apricot blouse with a distinctive pattern and a round neck. Her hair was tied back simply. 'Are you going to do it?'

'I don't know. I can't think straight!'

'Why don't you sit down and let me make you a cup of coffee? You could be more rational about things then.'

'I'm not being *irrational*,' Harriet said with extreme frustration. But she sat down and she didn't raise any obstacles when he got up to make the coffee.

And the wheels of her mind started to turn slowly rather than racing around uselessly.

It would be a solution.

It would provide not only the financial support she needed but, come to think of it, the moral support. She and Isabel had grown close. She also loved Heathcote. She was comfortable and secure here—and there were some marvellous paintings to work on when she finished her present job. Could she ask for more?

Despite her financial affairs being in much better repair thanks to Damien Wyatt's mother's treasures, once she wasn't earning, once she wasn't living rent free, living off her capital so to speak, she had a fair idea of how fast it would shrink.

But...

She looked across at his tall figure as he rounded up the coffee accoutrements, and had to marvel suddenly at how things had changed. How she'd hated him for his arrogance; how she'd hated the way he could kiss her without so much as a by-your-leave and leave her deeply moved. How she'd been so determined not to allow his effect on her to take root—only to discover that it had anyway.

But to discover at the same time why Damien Wyatt was so opposed to the concept of love ever after and the institution of marriage... A story that was painful even to think about.

She shivered suddenly and forced her mind away. And she asked herself if the wisest course of action for her peace of mind, if nothing else, was to go away from Heathcote as soon as she'd finished the first job.

But Brett! Brett—his name hammered in her mind. The more she could do for him, the more she could do to get him mobile again, the better and the sooner this nightmare would be over, for him as well as for her.

She held her peace for another couple of minutes until she had a steaming cup of Hawaiian coffee in front of her.

'I could do them,' she said slowly. 'The paintings. It would be one way to make sure Brett can stay on until his treatment is finished.'

'Good.' He said it briskly and in a way that gave her to understand it was a business deal between them and nothing more. And, before he could say any more, his phone rang.

'Excuse me, I'll take this downstairs; it's South Africa. Thank you for dinner, by the way.'

Harriet nodded and, moments later, she and Tottie were left alone.

'All sorted, Tottie.' Harriet dried sudden, ridiculous tears with her fingers. 'Dealt with, packed, labelled and filed away, that's me.'

She hugged Tottie then sat with her head in her hands for a while before she got up and resolutely put her kitchen to bed.

She was not to know that whilst Damien Wyatt might have sorted her out and locked her out of his life for the most part, his business life was about to become another matter. His PA, a man who'd worked closely with him for ten years, resigned out of the blue in order to train for his lifelong ambition—to climb Mount Everest.

If this wasn't trying enough, his South African trip was cancelled and the ramifications to his business empire as the lucrative business deal involved hung in the breeze were enough to make him extremely tense.

CHAPTER SIX

'TENSE, BLOODY-MINDED and all-round impossible,' Charlie said to Harriet one evening. 'That's Damien at the moment. It's like living under a thundercloud. I tell you what, I really feel for the poor sods he's interviewing for his PA position. I wonder if they have any idea what he might drive them to? I mean to say, it's got to be a pretty bizarre ambition, climbing Mount Everest.'

They were sharing what would have otherwise been a lonesome meal—Isabel was out and so was Damien.

Harriet had made hamburgers and chips, much to Charlie's approval.

Harriet had to laugh. 'I feel really guilty,

though,' she said as she passed the ketchup to Charlie.

'You!' He looked surprised.

'I…' She hesitated. 'It was because of me that he didn't go to Perth and on to South Africa. I can't help wondering if that…if that—' she gestured widely and shrugged '—caused all this.'

Charlie frowned. 'Why "because of you" didn't he go?'

'Well, he missed his flight to Perth because he came back to explain something.' Harriet bit her lip and berated herself for ever mentioning the matter but Charlie took issue with this.

'You can't open up a can of worms like that then play dumb,' he objected, 'but let me guess. You two had some sort of issue between you after my birthday party?'

Harriet sighed suddenly. 'Charlie, we've had issues between us since the day I smashed his car and his collarbone. Not to mention the day I slapped his face and he kissed me back. But his issues are…very complicated. And he wasn't supposed to be here while I finished the job,' she added, somewhat annoyed.

'Ah, well, so that explains—well, some of it! I didn't think some business deal hanging in the balance—I mean he's weathered a few of those before—was sufficient to cause this level of turmoil in my beloved brother.'

Harriet put her hands on her waist. 'That doesn't help me a lot, Charlie.'

'Or any of us! I think we'll just have to batten down the hatches and prepare for the worst. At least you can stay out of his way.'

This proved to be incorrect.

She was riding Sprite along Seven-mile Beach the next morning with Tottie at her stirrup. It was cool and crisp and the clarity of the air was amazing, dead flat calm water with hardly any surf, some pink clouds in a pale blue sky—and another horse riding towards her: Damien.

Her first thought was to gallop away in the opposite direction, and she started to do so but

Sprite was no match for his horse and he caught her up.

By this time, some common sense had returned to Harriet and she slowed Sprite to a walk.

'Morning, Harriet.'

She glanced across at him as Sprite jostled his big brown horse and Tottie looked relieved. 'Hi, Damien.' Their breath steamed in the early morning cool.

'Running away again?'

'I guess that was my first intention,' she confessed and found herself curiously unsettled. He looked so big in a khaki rain jacket and jeans with his dark head bare. Not at all cuddly, she reflected, not at all affected by the post dawn chill, whereas she was bundled up in a scarlet anorak, navy track pants and a scarlet beanie.

'Why?'

'I think,' she said carefully and straightened the reins through her fingers, 'we're all a little nervous around you at the moment.'

He grimaced. 'That bad?'

She nodded.

'Of course things haven't exactly gone my way lately, business-wise,' he observed as they turned their horses onto the path from the beach.

'I'm sorry if I was—unwittingly—in any way the cause of that.'

He looked across at her. 'You weren't. Although, of course, you are part of the overall problem. After you.' He indicated that she should precede him through the archway that led to Heathcote and the stables.

But she simply stared at him with her lips parted, her eyes incredulous, so Tottie took the initiative and Sprite followed.

And it wasn't until they got to the stables that they took up the thread of the conversation.

They tied their steaming horses beside each other in the wash bay.

'What overall problem?' she asked at last as she hosed Sprite down.

'The one I have with going into the lounge, for example.'

Harriet turned her hose off and took a metal scraper off its hook. 'Why should that be a problem?' She scraped energetically down Sprite's flank then ducked under her neck to do her other side.

'Well, if I'd flown halfway around the world and was in another country I might have found it easier to think of other things than you at Charlie's party. At the moment, every time I walk into the damn lounge it strikes me again.'

Harriet dropped the scraper and it clattered onto the concrete at the same as Sprite moved uneasily and her metal shoes also clattered on the concrete.

Damien stopped hosing his horse and came round to see if Harriet was all right.

'Fine. Fine!' She retrieved the scraper and handed it to him. 'I think I've finished.'

'Thanks.' He hung up his hose and started to use the scraper on his horse.

They worked in silence for a few minutes. Harriet rubbed Sprite down with a coarse towel then she inspected her feet and finally threw a rug over her. But all the time her mind was buzzing. How to deal with this? How to deal with the fact that she still felt incredibly guilty about how she'd fled at the end of Charlie's party after... after...

Even days later, her cheeks reddened at the thought of how abandoned—that was about the only way she could describe it—she'd felt and how she'd run like a scared rabbit.

She clicked her tongue and backed Sprite out of the wash bay to lead her to her box, where there was a feed already made up for her thanks to Stan.

Perhaps it was that feed waiting for her that made Sprite a bundle of impatience to get to her stall, but she suddenly put on a rare exhibition that would have done a buck jumper proud, an exhibition that scattered Tottie and even caused

Damien's horse, still tied in the wash bay, to try to rear and plunge.

'Sprite!' Harriet clung onto the lead with all her strength. 'Settle down, girl! What's got into you?'

'Tucker,' Damien said in her ear. 'I'll take her.'

And in a masterful display of horsemanship as well as strength, he calmed the mare down and got her into her box.

'Thank you! I was afraid I was going to lose her—another accident waiting to happen, to go down on my already tarnished record!' Harriet said breathlessly but whimsically.

Damien laughed as he came towards her out of the stable block and for an instant the world stood still for Harriet. He looked so alive and wickedly amused, so tall and dark, so sexy...

And what he did didn't help.

He came right up to her, slid his hands around her waist under her anorak and hugged her. 'I wouldn't have held that against you,' he said, holding her a little away.

Without thinking much about it, she put her hands on his shoulders. 'No?' She looked at him with mock scepticism.

'No. I would have laid the blame squarely at the horse's feet. She's always been a bit of a handful. Hence her name. Typical female,' he added.

'Damn!' Harriet assumed a self-righteous expression.

He raised an eyebrow.

'I was full of approval for you but you went and spoilt it with your anti-feminist remark!'

'My apologies, Miss Livingstone. Uh—how can I make amends? Let's see, you did pretty damn good for a girl before I took over and—can I cook you breakfast?'

Harriet blinked. 'You cook?'

He shrugged. 'Some things. Bacon and eggs.'

'Only bacon and eggs?'

'More or less. Steak, I do steak as well.'

'I have both,' Harriet said slowly.

He laughed again, kissed her fleetingly on the

lips, and removed his hands from her waist just as Stan came round the corner of the stables.

Fortunately Charlie turned up at the same time, wanting to know what all the hullabaloo was about and they repaired to the flat after Stan had offered to finish Damien's horse and put it in its box. And they had a jolly breakfast of steak, bacon and eggs.

Charlie even said, 'Notice how the sun's come out!'

Damien frowned. 'It's been up and out for a couple of hours.'

'I was speaking relatively,' Charlie said with dignity.

Damien narrowed his eyes as he studied his brother. 'I…think I get your drift,' he said slowly. 'My apologies.'

'That's all right. We'll forgive you, won't we, Harriet?'

She was clearing the table and about to pour the coffee but she couldn't help herself. She looked up and straight at Damien.

'Yes...' she said, but it sounded uncertain even to her own ears, nor could she mistake the ironic glint that came to his dark eyes as their gazes clashed.

So, she thought uneasily, he might laugh with me as he did this morning but I'm a long way from forgiven.

And although this lifting of the thundercloud, so to speak, over Heathcote, was much appreciated by Charlie and no doubt everyone else on the property, it brought Harriet mental anguish and confusion.

No longer was she able to keep Damien Wyatt on the back roads of her mind. Not that she'd been able to do that for a while but it seemed to have grown ten times worse day by day.

She was incredibly aware of him whenever he came within her orbit. He literally made her tremble inwardly and all her fine hairs rise. He made her tongue-tied now, never capable of thinking of anything to say.

He made the completion of the work on his
mother's treasures and the paintings drag because she spent a lot of time day-dreaming.

Would she ever finish this job? she asked herself desperately once.

Then the kitchen was finished and Isabel organised a party to celebrate the fact.

'I don't think I've ever seen a renovation,
especially not after a fire, be so swiftly and pain-
lessly achieved,' Harriet murmured to Isabel as
she was being given a tour of all the spectacu-
lar slimline stainless steel equipment and gran-
ite counters that now graced Heathcote's new
bottle-green, white and black kitchen.

'Ever *seen* a renovation after a fire?' Isabel
asked perkily.

'Well, no, but you know what I mean. By the
way, you sounded just like your nephew—your
older nephew,' she added.

Isabel laughed. 'Heaven forbid! Although he
has been pretty good lately. But if you really

want to know the reason for the speed and efficiency of this renovation, it's quite simple.'

'Your expert management of things?'

'Well, that too,' Isabel conceded. 'But it's money. It buys the best product, best workmen and in the long run it saves money.'

'Spoken like a true capitalist,' Harriet said but with affection.

'All right.' Isabel uncovered several platters on a long counter containing snacks. There were also plates and napkins plus bottles of champagne in ice buckets and gleaming glassware in amongst glorious vases of flowers.

'How many people have you asked?' Damien enquired as he pinched a smoked salmon savoury and had his hand slapped.

'Just the neighbours—don't,' Isabel replied.

'Just the neighbours!' Damien echoed. 'If you mean everyone we know around here that could be twenty to thirty.'

'Twenty-five. When has that ever been a problem?' Isabel enquired with her arms akimbo.

'Beloved, I was merely thinking that you must have done an awful lot of work. And I happen to know you don't like it.'

'Ah. I gave someone a trial run. She's applied for the cook's position. No, she's not here now,' she said as Damien looked around, 'but the proof will be in the pudding. There's plenty more to eat.'

One good thing about this party—people had been especially asked not to dress up since it was a kitchen party. So Harriet had been happy to attend in jeans and a lilac jumper. She'd been just as happy to leave after an hour although everyone else seemed to be content to stay on.

But it was a hollow feeling she encountered when she was upstairs in the flat. Hollow and lonely—hollow, ruffled and restless. And all due to watching Damien at his best.

Damien fascinating his neighbours with a blend of wit, seriousness, humour and setting not a few feminine pulses fluttering.

One of them was Penny Tindall, although

she'd fought to hide it, Harriet thought with some scorn.

She almost immediately took herself to task for this uncharitable thought, not only uncharitable towards Penny but investing herself with a superiority she did not possess. If she did she wouldn't be feeling miserable, lonely, stirred up and generally like crying herself to sleep all on Damien Wyatt's account, would she?

But she knew herself well enough to know that sleep would not come, so she took herself downstairs, closed herself into the studio, drew the curtains and sat down on a high stool. She'd just finished notating a beautiful ivory chess set and she pushed it aside to study an object she wasn't all too sure about.

It resembled some giant curved tooth set on a brass base and embellished with scrimshaw of African wildlife—an elephant, a rhino, a lion, a cheetah and a buffalo.

She was handling it, turning it this way and

that, when the door clicked open and Damien stood there.

They simply stared at each other for a long moment then he said, 'Can I come in?'

'Of course.' Harriet slipped off her stool and pushed her hair behind her ears. 'I...I...'

'Kitchen parties are not your cup of tea?' he suggested as he closed the door behind him.

'No. I mean...I haven't got anything against them really.' She grimaced. 'That sounds a bit weird.'

He didn't agree or disagree. He simply looked at her with patent amusement. Then he looked at the objects on the table and noticed the chess set.

'I was wondering where that had got to,' he commented. 'Charlie and Mum used to play a lot of chess. Charlie is a bit of a genius at it. Do you play?' He lifted a king, rotated it then set it down.

She nodded.

'Well?'

'Well enough.'

He studied her narrowly. 'Why do I get the feeling that's the guarded sort of response someone who is sensational at something gives you just before they set out to fleece you shamelessly?'

Harriet maintained a grave, innocent expression—for about half a minute, then she had to grin.

'You look like the proverbial Cheshire Cat,' he drawled. 'Did I hit the nail on the head?'

'I'm not bad at chess,' she confessed. 'I used to play with my father.'

'Don't think Charlie has had time to play for years.' He moved on and picked up the tooth-like object she'd been handling.

'Hello!' he said, as he picked it up. 'Haven't seen you for years!'

Harriet's eyes widened. 'You know it?'

'Sure,' he said easily. 'My mother showed it to me when she got it.'

Harriet's eyes widened further. 'So you know what it is?'

'Uh-huh. Don't you?'

'No. Well, a tooth of some kind from a whale maybe, but I can't find any paperwork that goes with it so I'm a little frustrated.'

He picked it up again. 'It's a tusk—a warthog tusk.'

Harriet's mouth fell open. 'Seriously?'

'Seriously. My mother was quite taken with African artefacts.'

Harriet frowned. 'Where are they?'

'Haven't you come across any more of them?'

'No. Apart from this, nothing.'

He sat down on the corner of the table. 'We'll have to consult Isabel.'

Harriet stared at the warthog tusk with its delicate scrimshaw. 'We'll have to get in an African expert,' she said.

'Couldn't you look it up?'

Harriet shrugged. 'Perhaps. How many do you think she had?'

'Hundreds,' he replied.

Harriet paled. 'But…that might mean I could be here for the next ten years!'

'Now that,' he agreed with a grin, 'could be a problem. Talk about growing old on the job.' But he sobered as she moved restlessly. 'Not to mention the other complications it would cause.' And the way his gaze roamed up and down her figure gave her no doubt that he meant complications in an extremely personal way.

'Uh—look, I'll think about it tomorrow,' she said hastily. 'Right now I should probably go to bed. I'll need—' she smiled shakily '—all my resources tomorrow if I'm to track down hundreds of things like warthog tusks.'

She laid the tusk back in its box, briefly tidied the table top, and came purposefully round the table towards the door.

Damien uncoiled his lean length from the stool and barred her way. 'Am I getting my marching orders, Miss Livingstone?' he said softly.

Her eyes flew to his. 'This was *your* idea—'

She stopped abruptly and could have kicked herself.

'Mmm…' He scanned the way her breasts were heaving beneath the lilac wool. 'My idea for us to desist? So it was, but are you claiming you had another direction in mind for us?'

'No. I mean—' she bit her lip '—I don't know of any other way there could be and that's sad but probably a blessing in the long run.'

He put his arms around her. 'I didn't mean to make you sad. I could so easily…turn things around. Like this.'

His kiss, and although she'd known it was coming she did nothing about it, was like a balm to her soul.

She no longer felt hollow and lonely and restless. She felt quite different. Smooth and silken as his hands roamed beneath her jumper and his lips moved from hers to the hollows at the base of her throat to the soft spot where her shoulder curved into her neck.

Then he took her by surprise. He lifted her up

and sat her on the table and she wound her legs around him—to have him grin wickedly down at her.

'If you only knew what your legs do to me,' he murmured, and his hands moved up to cup her breasts.

Harriet paused what she was doing, running her hands over the hard wall of his chest, and rested her hands on his shoulders. And she tensed.

'What?' he asked, his eyes suddenly narrowing.

'Someone coming,' she breathed and pushed him away so she could slide off the table and re-arrange her clothes.

'Someone's always bloody coming,' he grated.

But whoever had been coming changed their mind and the footsteps receded.

Harriet let out a quivering breath.

'Would it matter if anyone saw us?' he asked abruptly.

She stirred. 'Surely it would complicate things

even more?' She laced her fingers together. 'Damien…' She closed her eyes briefly. 'I'm sorry this happened. I'm sorry it keeps happening but if there's no future for us, if you're sure, I need—I need to go away from Heathcote.' Silent tears were suddenly coursing down her cheeks. She scrubbed at them impatiently. 'I have nearly finished your mother's things but if there are hundreds more…' She gestured helplessly. 'And the paintings. I don't see how I can stay. Surely you m-must—' her voice cracked '—agree?'

He took in her tear-streaked face and the anguish in her eyes. And for a moment a terrible temptation to say *Stay somehow we'll work it out, Harriet* rose in him. But another side of him refused to do it, a side that recalled all too clearly and bitterly how he'd been cheated and made a fool of…

'I'm sorry,' he said. 'This is my fault, what happened here tonight, not yours. It won't happen again, so please stay. Goodnight.'

He touched her wet cheek with his fingertips then he was gone.

Harriet took herself up to her flat and cried herself to sleep.

A week later their truce had held. Not that Damien had spent much time at Heathcote. But they were able to interact normally, or so she thought. As in the instance when she was explaining to him about his mother's artefacts.

'Isabel forgot to tell me,' she told him.

He lifted an eyebrow. 'What?'

'Oh, sorry, I should have started at the beginning. Your mother sold all her artefacts just before she…er…passed away. Somehow or other, the warthog tusk must have been overlooked.'

Damien grimaced and folded his arms across his chest. 'No doubt to your great relief.'

'Mostly,' Harriet said. 'I have to admit the thought of becoming an expert on apes and ivory et cetera was a little daunting.'

'Apes and ivory?'

'It comes from the Bible—Kings, First Book, chapter ten, verse twenty-two. *"...the navy of Tharshish bringing gold, and silver, ivory, and apes, and peacocks."* From Africa to King Solomon.'

'How did you come by that?' he queried.

'I did *some* research. It's fascinating.'

He studied her. She was now writing with her head bent and her expression absorbed. As usual, Tottie was lying at her feet. Her hair was loose and curly and she wore tartan trews and a cream cable stitch sweater. She looked at home on this cool autumn evening.

And if she wasn't close to becoming a part of Heathcote she wasn't far from it—or was she already? he wondered.

And was he mad not to make sure she stayed?

At the same moment his phone rang. He pulled it out of his pocket and studied it with a frown then he answered it tersely. 'Wyatt.'

Harriet looked up and she tensed as he said,

'*What*?' and 'When and where?' in hard, clipped, disbelieving tones.

And she realised he'd gone pale and his knuckles around the phone were white, and a feeling of dread started to grip her although she had no idea what news he was getting.

Then he ended the call and threw his phone down.

'What?' she asked huskily. 'Something's happened.'

She saw his throat working and he closed his eyes briefly. 'Charlie,' he said hoarsely at last. 'His plane's gone down. Somewhere in the north of Western Australia. They either can't be more specific or it's classified information.'

He sat down and dropped his face into his hands then looked up. 'It's rugged terrain if it's the Kimberley. Rivers, gorges.' He drew a deep breath then crashed his fist on the table so that her coffee mug jumped and spilt. 'And there's nothing I can do.'

'I'm so sorry,' Harriet murmured and slid her

hand across the table to cover his. 'I'm sure they'll be doing all they can.'

'There must be *something* I can do!' There was frustration written into the lines and angles of his face. He got up and looked around as if he had no idea where he was. He said, 'Excuse me, Harriet, but I can do more from my study and my computer.'

She rose hastily. 'Of course. I'll bring you a nightcap in a while if you like.' But she didn't think he'd even heard her as he loped down the stairs two at a time with Tottie hard on his heels.

Harriet marvelled at the dog's sensitivity; she obviously had no doubt where she was needed most tonight.

And to keep herself occupied and keep at bay images of a fiery crash and Charlie's broken body, she went downstairs to the studio to do some work of her own.

She was cleaning a delicate china figurine with a cotton bud dipped in a weak solution when Isabel, looking as if she'd aged ten years in the space of a few hours, came over from the big house.

'Any news?' Harriet asked.

Isabel shook her head and pulled out a stool. And she hugged her mohair stole around her.

'How's Damien?'

Isabel shook her head. 'He's…it'll kill him to lose Charlie. Me too, but more so Damien. They're really close, despite the way they josh each other. They got even closer after what happened with Veronica and Patrick.' Isabel stopped self-consciously.

'He's told me about her. So Patrick was the baby?'

'Uh-huh.' Isabel touched a finger to the figurine Harriet had finished cleaning and had dried. 'Hello, I remember you,' she said to it and again looked self-conscious. 'You must think I'm crazy,' she said to Harriet this time, 'but I do remember this figurine. It always sat on its own little circular table in the upstairs hall. That's where Damien's mother always kept it, but Veronica…' She trailed off.

Harriet said nothing.

Isabel shrugged. 'I don't know why I shouldn't tell you, seeing as you know some of it. It also helps to think of something else. If you've wondered why a lot of this stuff was more or less hidden, that was Veronica's doing. She didn't like antiques or objets d'art. A very modern girl was our Veronica, in more ways than one.' Isabel's tone was loaded with disapproval. 'Mind you,' she added, 'Damien said no to a lot of her plans for the modernisation of Heathcote.'

But then she sighed. 'One should never pass judgement on relationships because it's almost impossible to know the full story. And it's hard not to be biased, anyway.'

'How old is Patrick now?' Harriet asked.

'Let's see—nearly three.'

'I don't suppose Damien has any reason to have any contact with him?' She rinsed out a couple of cloths and suspended them from pegs from a dryer over the sink.

'No. Well, not directly.'

Harriet washed her hands and stood drying them on a red and white checked towel as a frown grew in her eyes.

'He and Charlie worked out a plan. Because things are and always will be pretty tense between Veronica and Damien, I imagine—and because I can't quite hide my feelings—' Isabel grimaced '—Charlie sees Patrick fairly frequently. To make sure he's OK and to give him a constant man in his life, I guess you could say. Charlie somehow or other had a better understanding of Veronica than me or Damien. That sounds odd.' Isabel gestured a little helplessly.

'I don't think so. I think that's…Charlie,' Harriet said slowly. 'I wouldn't be surprised if Charlie keeps a sort of weather eye out for Damien.'

'Oh, I think he does.' Isabel rested her chin in her hands and studied Harriet. 'You're pretty perceptive yourself, my dear.'

Harriet grimaced. 'I don't know about that. So she—Veronica—didn't marry Patrick's father?'

Isabel shook her head. 'She hasn't remarried.'

'Is there any chance of them getting back together?'

'No.' Isabel said it quite definitely. 'It was one of those white-hot affairs that was too explosive to last, even apart from the drama over Patrick. Of course the double, triple even quadruple irony to it all is that Patrick was named after my father, Damien's grandfather.'

Harriet let the towel drop onto the counter. 'Oh, no!'

'Oh, yes.' Isabel shrugged. 'Not that there would be any point in changing his name and he'd been christened by the time they found out, anyway. But it does…it was such a mess.'

Harriet sat down. 'Do you think he'll ever marry again?'

Isabel stretched then she rocked Harriet to the core. 'Yes. If *you* would have him.'

CHAPTER SEVEN

'I...I BEG YOUR pardon?' Harriet stammered.

But Isabel simply looked at her wisely.

Harriet got up and did a turn around the studio with her arms crossed almost protectively. 'It couldn't work. The reason he came back from Perth—not that he ever got there—was to tell me why it couldn't work.'

'Why couldn't it?'

'He doesn't want to be married again. He's suspicious and cynical now and, even without any of that, he's a difficult, unbending kind of person and he admits that his habit of command was probably one of the reasons they fell out so badly.'

'Probably,' Isabel conceded. 'He's very much like my father, his grandfather, the first Patrick.

The one who started it all. Dynamic, forceful—'
Isabel nodded wryly '—difficult. Whereas my
brother, Damien's father, was more interested
in culture and the arts, passionate about sailing, that kind of thing. He was so nice—' Isabel looked fond '—but it's true to say we went
backwards during his stewardship and it took
all of Damien's grandfather's genes plus plenty
of his own kind of steely determination to pull
the business out of that slump.'

'The first thing that struck me about him,'
Harriet said dryly, 'was how arrogant he was.
I never felt more…more vindicated—that's not
the right word, but it definitely was a release of
some kind—when I slapped his face, although
I got myself kissed for my pains.' She stopped
and bit her lip.

'That first day you came to Heathcote?' Isabel
queried and when Harriet nodded she laughed.

'Sorry,' she said, 'but I knew something had
happened between you two. So did Charlie.'

'Charlie walked in on it,' Harriet said gloomily, 'that's how he knew.' Then she had to smile. 'If you could have seen his expression.'

But her smile faded and she put a hand to her mouth. 'Oh, God, please let him be OK!'

Isabel got up and came to put her arms around Harriet. 'I think we should go to bed. There's nothing we can do tonight. Goodnight, my dear.'

'Goodnight,' Harriet whispered back.

But, back up in the flat, Harriet had no desire to go to bed, she discovered, and not only on Charlie's account, although that feeling of dread was still running through her.

It was Isabel's bombshell that she also had on her mind. It was the fact that she'd been able to see it was no use denying to Isabel that she was helplessly, hopelessly in love with her nephew.

But how had she given herself away? She'd only admitted it to herself recently. Of course it had been bubbling away for longer than that; she just hadn't been aware of it.

'I must be incredibly transparent,' she murmured aloud. 'Maybe I do go around with my head in the clouds. Perhaps I was unaware of how I reacted when his name came up? Or perhaps Isabel and Charlie had been comparing notes? Did they see something in Damien, both of us, they hadn't expected to see?'

She shook her head and, with a heavy sigh, decided to take him a cup of cocoa.

What if he doesn't like cocoa? she immediately asked herself. He doesn't drink tea. They couldn't be less alike, tea and cocoa, however, but, if he needs some fortitude, what better than, say, an Irish coffee?

She found him in his study, staring out of the window.

The breeze had dropped and the sky had cleared so there was starlight on the water and a pale slice of moon.

He didn't move when she knocked softly; she didn't think he'd heard her.

She put the tray with two Irish coffees on his

desk and walked over to him, making sure she approached from a wide angle so as not to startle him.

'Any news?' she asked.

He turned his head. 'No.'

'I brought us some—liquid fortitude.' She gestured to the tall glasses on the tray.

He glanced at them and sketched a smile—and held out his hand to her.

She hesitated for one brief moment then she took it, knowing full well what was going to happen and knowing at the same time it was the least she could do for him because it all but broke her heart to see the suffering etched into his expression.

And she went into his arms with no hesitation at all. But he surprised her. He held her loosely and some of the lines left his face as he said, with a quirk of humour, 'There is something you could always put down on the plus side for me.'

'What?' she breathed, as his nearness started to overwhelm her.

'I'm taller.'

Her lips curved. 'Yes. You are.'

He raised a hand and traced the line of her jaw. 'Does it help? Or do you prefer your men shorter?'

'I do not,' she observed seriously. 'They make me feel like an Amazon. No, it's definitely a plus.'

'Good. I mean that makes me feel good. I was beginning to develop an inferiority complex. Not that I'll ever be able to even up the ledger.' He took a very deep breath. 'I'm talking nonsense but—what will I do without Charlie if it goes that way?'

Harriet slipped her arms around him and laid her head on his chest. 'Don't think like that. It hasn't happened yet, it may not happen.'

'It's so vast up there and if it's not dry and desolate, the shores and the creeks have crocodiles—I know, I've been fishing up there.' His arms tightened around her.

'But they must have very sophisticated tracking and search and rescue equipment. Don't give up hope.'

'You sound so sensible and sane. And you feel so good,' he added barely audibly.

'So…so do you,' she murmured back and raised her mouth for his kiss.

'This is getting out of hand,' he said some time later as they drew apart to take deep breaths and steady themselves. 'I hope you don't mind me doing this.'

Harriet regarded him gravely. 'It did annoy me, the last time.'

His eyebrows shot up? 'How come?'

She chuckled. 'You never asked me for my preferences in the matter. You just went ahead and did it.'

'Miss Livingstone,' he said formally, 'please tell me what your preferences are in the mat-ter—*this* matter. So as not to be misunderstood.' He pulled her closer and cradled her hips to him.

Harriet took an unsteady breath. 'They appear

LINDSAY ARMSTRONG 205

to be very similar to yours in this instance.' And she linked her arms around his neck and stared into his eyes.

It was a long, compelling look they shared and Harriet strove to convey the sense that she understood his need and the starkness of his emotions and that she wanted to offer him some comfort.

He breathed urgently and said one word. 'Sure?'

'Sure,' she answered.

He looked around and gestured at the large comfortable settee. 'Here?'

'If you don't have a haystack or a loft?' she queried with laughter glinting in her eyes.

'I...' He hesitated then he saw that glint of laughter and for a moment his arms around her nearly crushed her.

'All right,' he said into her hair, and that was the last word spoken for a while.

But what followed didn't stop Harriet from thinking along the lines of, *I was right. I sensed that he'd know how to make love to a woman in a way that would thrill her and drive her to excesses she didn't know she could reach...*

Because that was exactly what happened to her. From a fairly timid lover—she suddenly realised this with a pang of embarrassment—she became a different creature.

She craved his hands on her body. She helped him to take her clothes off and she gloried in the way he touched and stroked her. She became impatient to help him shed his clothes.

She made no effort to hide her excitement as they lay together on the settee and he cupped her breasts and plucked her nipples, as he drew his fingers ever lower down her body.

And she clung to him as desire took her by storm and there was only one thing she craved— to be taken. So she moved provocatively against him and did her own fingertip exploration of him until he growled and turned her onto her back and made sure she was ready for him, then they were united in an urgent rhythm and finally an explosion of sensation.

'Oh!' she breathed, as she arched her body against him.

And he buried his head between her breasts as he shuddered to a final closure.

'Harriet?'

'Mmm…?'

'All right?'

'Oh yes.' Her eyes remained closed but she smiled a secret little smile.

He grinned and dropped the lightest kiss on her hair. 'Wait here.'

She moved in an urgent little protest. 'Don't go away.'

'I'll be right back.' But he checked his phone and glanced at his computer screen before he went out.

She looked a question at him but he shook his head.

And he was as good as his word; he was back

in a couple of minutes with a sheet, a blanket and a couple of pillows. He'd also put on a pair of shorts.

He covered her and made sure she was comfortable.

Then he stopped. 'There are six bedrooms we could go to. I'm not sure why we didn't in the first place.'

'We weren't in the most practical frame of mind,' she suggested.

He sat down beside her and smoothed her hair. 'If I recall correctly, you were even talking about haystacks.'

'Silly talk.' She slipped her hand under her cheek. 'Love talk. Well—' she bit her lip '—you know what I mean—pillow talk, that's it!'

'Yes.'

Did he say it too soon? she immediately found herself wondering.

'Your Dutch courage drinks have gone cold,' he added.

Harriet grimaced.

'I'll get us something else.' He pushed his phone into his pocket.

'Don't.' Harriet sat up and pulled the sheet up. 'I mean, don't wake Isabel. She could be shocked even if she does think…' She broke off and hoped he didn't see the colour she felt rising in her cheeks.

But he appeared to notice nothing as he said, 'Isabel has her own apartment downstairs. It closes off and she doesn't hear a thing. I won't be long. Don't—' his lips twisted '—go anywhere.'

She didn't go anywhere but she did pull her knickers and her shirt on.

It wasn't brandy, as she'd been expecting, that he brought back—it was a bottle of champagne.

Harriet studied the dark green bottle with its gold foil and the two tall glasses on the tray that he deposited on his desk. 'Should we?' she asked tentatively. 'In the circumstances?'

His hair was hanging in his eyes. All he wore

were shorts but he could hardly have been more magnificent as he picked up the champagne bottle, Harriet thought as she caught her breath. His shoulders were broad, his chest was sprinkled with dark hair, his diaphragm was flat, his legs long and strong. He was beautiful, she thought with a pang. How was she ever going to forget him…?

'In the circumstances,' he said as he unwound the wire around the cork, 'there is not only you and me to celebrate, there's Charles Walker Wyatt. Wherever you are, Charlie, may you be safe and sound!'

He popped the cork and poured the two glasses. He handed one to Harriet and clinked his against hers. 'Charlie,' he said.

'Charlie,' Harriet echoed. 'May you be safe and sound!'

His phone buzzed. He grabbed it and studied the screen, and breathed a huge sigh of relief as he read the message.

'They've found him. They've found the site

where it came down and the crew are all alive. Charlie has a broken arm and leg and a few gashes but otherwise he's mostly OK.'

Harriet flew off the settee into his arms. 'Oh, thank heavens! Do you think they heard us, whoever is in charge of these things up there? I mean in heaven as well as North Western Australia? I think they must have!'

He laughed down at her. 'You could be right.'

'Where is he?'

'They're taking him to Darwin Hospital. They'll keep him there for a few weeks. Where's your glass?'

'Here.' She went to retrieve it from the end table beside the settee and he held it steady in her hand while he refilled it.

Then he looked down at her and raised an eyebrow. 'So—I'm over and done with, am I?'

Harriet looked down at herself. 'Not at all,' she denied. 'I just felt a little—undressed.' She grimaced. 'Not that I'm particularly—overdressed at the moment.'

'Stay like that,' he advised. 'Because I'll be right back. I'll just pass on the news to Isabel.'

She was sitting on the settee with the sheet covering her legs when he came back. He brought his glass over and sat down beside her. He dropped his arm over her shoulders.

'Cheers!'

'Cheers!' She sipped her champagne then laid her head on his shoulder. 'Any particular person in mind this time?'

'Yes.' He drew his hand through her hair. 'Us.'

'Well, we've both got brothers on the mend, so yes—to us!'

'True,' he agreed, 'but I meant a toast to what just happened here on this settee between us and the hope that it may continue to happen for us, not necessarily in a study or a haystack—a bed would do,' he said with a glint of humour. 'In other words, when will you marry me, Harriet Livingstone?'

Harriet, in the echoing silence that followed

his words, asked herself why she should not have expected this. Because he'd *told* her he could never overcome the cynicism he'd been left with after the debacle of his first marriage?

'Harriet?' He removed his arm and put his fingers beneath her chin to turn her face to his. 'What?'

Her eyes were wide but dark and very blue. 'You said…' she began quietly.

'Forget what I said earlier,' he ordered. 'Have you never said or done something and almost immediately started to wonder why you did it?' He didn't wait for an answer. 'Well, I have and that was one of them. Anyway, things have changed.'

'Nothing's changed,' she denied.

'There you go again,' he drawled. 'You kissed me once and were all set to walk away from me. Don't tell me that modus operandi extends to making love to me as if—' he paused, and looked deep into her eyes '—your soul depended on it, then walking away?'

Harriet breathed heavily with great frustration. 'I don't have a "modus operandi" I employ like that,' she said through her teeth.

'So why did you make love to me like that?'

She opened her mouth then gestured, annoyed. 'I felt sorry for you—I felt sorry for *me*. It was so lonely and scary not knowing what had happened to Charlie; it was awful. That's—' she lifted her chin '—why I did it.'

'There had to be more than that.'

Harriet moved restlessly then she sighed. 'Yes. Of course. We obviously—' she shrugged '—are attracted.'

'Thank you,' he said with considerable irony. 'So why's it such a bad idea? We both appeared,' he said dryly, 'to have forgotten our inhibitions and our hang-ups as well.'

Harriet acknowledged this with a tinge of colour mounting in her cheeks but she said, 'Temporarily, yes, but you can't spend your life in bed. And I get the feeling marriage can create a pressure cooker environment for those hang-ups if they're still lingering.'

'Don't,' he advised, 'come the philosopher with me, Harriet Livingstone.'

She bristled. 'Don't be ridiculous! It's only common sense.'

He grinned fleetingly. 'OK. How about this, then? If you won't marry me, would you consider a relationship? That should give our hang-ups the freedom to rattle in the breeze rather than build up all sorts of pressure.'

Harriet sat up. 'No, I will not! And I'll tell you why. You've got me on your conscience again, haven't you? You couldn't change so suddenly otherwise. Well, you don't need to. I'll be fine.'

He sat up, all trace of amusement gone. 'Listen,' he said harshly, 'if I have got you on my conscience, I've got good reason. You came here to Heathcote obviously traumatised—I wouldn't be surprised if you were traumatised the day you ran into me. You were as skinny as a rake—and all because some guy had passed you over for another girl—'

'Not just another girl,' Harriet threw in. 'My best friend.'

Damien paused.

'Someone I loved and trusted,' she went on. 'We met in our last year at school. I hadn't made any close friends up until then because we moved around so much. That's why I think she meant so much to me. Then Carol and I went to the same college and we did everything together. We backpacked around Europe. We did a working holiday on a cattle station; we did so much together.

'And all the while we dated guys, but not terribly seriously until I met Simon and she met Peter. And for a few months we double-dated. But then we drifted apart. Simon and I were talking marriage. Carol and Pete weren't so serious.' She stopped and shrugged.

'And then Simon wasn't so serious,' Damien contributed.

Harriet nodded. 'I think Carol tried to avoid it but it didn't work. And *they* got married. So you see, it was a double betrayal. That's what made it so painful. And in the midst of it all my father died and my brother had this accident…and…I was alone. Everything that meant the most to me was gone or, if not gone, terribly injured. I don't know how I got myself together but, once I did, I decided I was the only one I could rely on.'

'I see—I do see,' he said gently.

'And it's not something I want to go through again, any kind of a betrayal. And that's why—' she turned to Damien '—I'm not prepared to marry you or be your mistress because you've got me on your conscience.'

'I—'

'No.' She put her hand over his. 'I'm certainly not prepared to fall in love with you, only to find you don't trust me, to find you don't and never will believe in love ever after.'

'What you need,' he said after a long, painful pause, 'is someone like Charlie.'

Harriet jumped in astonishment.

'I don't mean Charlie per se,' he continued, looking annoyed with himself. 'I mean someone uncomplicated, with no hang-ups and no habit of command. No back story.'

He pushed the sheet aside and stood up.

Harriet stared up at him, her lips parted, her eyes questioning. 'What…what's going to happen now?' she queried unevenly.

Damien Wyatt looked down at her and his lips twisted. 'Nothing.'

'Nothing,' she echoed.

'What did you expect?'

'I…I don't know,' she stammered.

'That I'd kick you out?'

'Well, no. I mean—not precisely.' Harriet reached for her pedal pushers and stepped into them.

'I'll be off to Darwin first thing tomorrow and I'll stay with Charlie for as long as he needs me. Then—' he grimaced '—I'll rearrange my

Africa trip. Whilst you can finish my mother's things and start on the paintings.'

'I'm not sure if I can do that.'

'You should. I'm sure it'll do your brother good to have you around.'

Harriet bit her lip.

He watched her intently.

She became conscious of his scrutiny. And it seemed to bring back the whole incredible sequence of events as they'd unfolded in this very room, not the least her passionate response to his lovemaking. It did more than that. It awoke tremors of sensation down her body and a sense of longing in her heart—a longing to be in his arms, a longing to be safe with him, a longing to be beloved...

She closed her eyes briefly because, of course, that wasn't going to happen. All the same, how to leave him?

'I don't know what to say,' she murmured.

'Not easy.' A smile appeared fleetingly in his eyes. 'Thanks but no thanks?' he suggested.

Harriet flinched.

'Or maybe just, from me, anyway—take care?' he mused. 'Yes, in your case, Harriet Livingstone, I think that's particularly appropriate. Don't drive into any more Aston Martins, or anything, for that matter; you take care now. By the way, if there are any consequences you wouldn't be so head-in-the-clouds as not to let me know?'

Harriet took a sobbing little breath, grabbed her shoes and ran past him out of the door.

CHAPTER EIGHT

'HARRIET, YOU'RE WORKING your fingers to the bone!' Isabel Wyatt accused as she stood in the studio doorway, shaking raindrops off her umbrella a couple of weeks later. 'It's Sunday,' she continued. 'Even if you're not religious, you need a rest. What is the matter?'

'Nothing! Come in. I'll make you a cuppa. I'm just working on the Venetian masks. It's a pity they got so dusty. Look at this lovely Columbina!'

Harriet held up a white porcelain half-mask studded with glittering stones and dyed feathers.

'Where does the name come from?'

'A Columbina is a stock character in Italian comedy, usually a maid who's—' Harriet shrugged '—a gossip, flirty, a bit of a wag and in English known as a soubrette.'

'Obviously not above disguising herself with a mask for the purpose of delicious secret liaisons,' Isabel said.

Harriet paused her dusting operation as the word *liaison* struck a chord with her, and for a moment she wanted to run away to the end of the earth as she thought of Damien Wyatt.

But she forced herself to take hold.

'Something like that,' she murmured. 'There are examples in this collection of all the different materials used to make masks, did you know? Leather, for example.' She held up a mask. 'Porcelain, as in the Columbina, and of course glass. Did you know the Venice Carnival goes back to 1162, when the Serenissima, as she was known then, defeated the Patriarch of Aquileila?'

'I did know that bit, as a matter of fact.' Isabel took the leather mask from Harriet. 'I've been to the Venice Carnival. It was also outlawed by the King of Austria in 1797 but no one knows exactly what prompted the population of Venice to be so exceedingly taken up with disguising themselves. Come along.'

'Where?'

'Upstairs to your kitchen, where *I* will make you a cuppa. Now don't argue with me, Harriet Livingstone!'

'What happened?' Isabel asked about twenty minutes later when they both had steaming mugs of tea in front of them on the refectory table as well as a plate of rich, bursting with cherries fruitcake.

'You mean…?' Harriet looked a question at Isabel.

'I mean with you and Damien—I'm not a fool, Harriet,' Isabel warned. 'Look, I wasn't going to say anything but you're so obviously…upset.'

Harriet frowned. 'We wouldn't suit, that's all.'

'And that's why you've been working all hours of the day and night and looking all haunted and pale?' Isabel looked at her sardonically.

'I need to get this job finished,' Harriet said

sharply. 'It's really started to drag—I just couldn't seem to get on top of it! Even the kitchen's been rebuilt whilst I didn't seem to be getting much further forward! But I need to put Heathcote behind me and I wish I'd never laid eyes on Damien Wyatt.'

'I'm glad you didn't say all the Wyatts.' Isabel stared at her.

Harriet looked away. 'I'm sorry. No, of course not you, Isabel. Or Charlie. But, ideally, I'd like to be gone before Damien and Charlie get home from Darwin. Look—' she turned back to Damien's aunt '—it's impossible for us to be in the same place now. Believe me.'

Isabel opened her mouth, hesitated, then said, 'So you're not going to do the paintings?'

'I…I…no.'

'How about your brother?'

Harriet licked her lips. 'He's making…progress.' But of course Brett was at the back of her mind, and how much easier it would be to make ends meet if she did stay on and do the paintings. But all the guilt in the world associated with Brett couldn't make her stay, not now, not after...

She sighed inwardly and pushed the plate of fruitcake towards Isabel. 'I made it to welcome Charlie home,' she said desolately and stood up abruptly to cross over to the window and stare out at the dismal, rainswept landscape. 'He loves fruitcake.'

'They'll be home shortly.'

'Autumn has come with a vengeance,' Brett said.

Harriet huddled inside her coat and agreed with him.

They were outside, despite the chill—Brett loved being outdoors whenever he could so she'd pushed him in his wheelchair to a sheltered arbour in the grounds. The breeze, however, had found its way around the arbour and it wasn't as sheltered as she'd thought it would be.

'I want to show you something,' he said.

Harriet looked enquiring and hoped he didn't

notice that she was preoccupied but she couldn't seem to help herself. She was not only preoccupied but she was trying to dredge up the courage to tell him she was going back to Sydney…

'Here.' He took the rug she'd insisted on draping over his legs and handed it to her.

'Oh, I'm all right,' she protested.

'Actually, you look half-frozen,' he responded with a grin, 'but all I want you to do is hold it for a couple of minutes.'

And, so saying, he levered himself out of the wheelchair and, with a stiff, slightly jerky gait but, all the same, walked around the arbour completely unaided and came to stand in front of her.

Harriet's mouth had fallen open and her eyes were huge.

'What do you think of that?' he asked with obvious pride.

Harriet jumped up and flung her arms around him. 'Oh, Brett,' she cried joyfully. 'That's such an improvement! When? How? Why? I mean…'

She stopped. 'You've been holding out on me!' she told him.

'Yes. I wanted it to be a big surprise.' He hugged her back then rocked slightly. 'There's still a way to go, though.'

'Sit down, sit down,' she insisted immediately, 'and tell me all about it. I think I can guess a bit of it, though. Your new physiotherapist?'

Brett sat down in his chair and nodded. 'Yes. Ellen has made a huge difference, but not only as a physio. She—' he paused '—she got me talking. See, I seemed to reach a plateau that I couldn't get beyond and she asked me one day if there was anything I was worried about, other than the obvious. And I found that there was and it was something that made me feel helpless and hopeless.'

'What?' Harriet asked fearfully.

He smiled at her and put his hand over hers. 'You,' he said simply.

Harriet gasped.

'Because of all the things you gave up for me,'

he said. 'Because I didn't know how I could ever repay you. Because I didn't much like the sound of this guy you went to work for but there was not a damn thing I could do about it.'

'Oh, Brett!'

'And somehow I found myself telling Ellen all this—she said the best thing I could do for you was to walk again. It just seemed—' he shook his head '—to put the fire back into me,' he marvelled. 'But there's still a way to go.'

'And will Ellen be with you down that road?' Harriet asked.

'I think so. I hope so. She…we—' he managed to look embarrassed and uplifted at the same time '—really get along.'

Harriet hugged him again. 'I'm so glad. So glad,' she repeated, 'because I'm going back to Sydney tomorrow. I know, I know,' she said to his look of surprise, 'it's a bit out of the blue but I've finished the job at last! And I'd like to look around for another one. Also, I told you about his brother?' Brett nodded. 'Well, they're due home from Darwin in a couple of days and it'll be a family time, I'm sure.'

Brett stared at her. 'What's he done to you?'

'Done?' She blinked.

'Yep,' Brett said grimly. 'Damien Wyatt.'

'Nothing! He's been quite—he's been quite kind, all things considered—'

'Don't give me that, Harry,' Brett said concernedly. 'I can see with my own eyes that you look all haunted.'

Harriet put a hand to her mouth. 'Do I really—? I mean, am I really that easy to read—? I mean—'

'Yes, you are. For someone who goes into her own little world quite frequently, you're amazingly easy to read,' he said somewhat dryly.

Harriet bit her lip then took a deep breath. 'If there's any trauma, he didn't cause it,' she said. 'I did. And I want you to believe that and—' she stood up '—I want you to put it out of your mind and continue this…this marvellous recovery. Ellen is right, you see; it's the *very* best thing you could do for me.'

'I can't let you go like this,' Isabel said the next morning as she watched Harriet pack her stuff into Brett's battered old four-wheel drive. 'Damien will never forgive me!'

It was another blustery autumn day.

'Stop worrying about it,' Harriet advised her. 'Between the two of you, you'll have enough on your minds helping Charlie to get better without worrying about me. Besides which, I'm not that bad a driver,' she added with some asperity.

'There could be differing views on the matter.' Isabel looked mutinous. 'Look, take the Holden!'

'I couldn't possibly take the Holden,' Harriet argued. 'It doesn't belong to me!'

'Ah!' Isabel pounced on an idea. 'It could be said to belong to *me*, however!'

Harriet didn't stop packing up her vehicle.

'What I mean is,' Isabel continued, 'I have a

share in Heathcote, which includes all the equipment and machinery, so I am able, equally, to dispose of—things. Therefore I can gift you the blue Holden!' she finished triumphantly. 'Isn't that how they phrase it these days?'

Harriet put the last of her bags into the four-wheel drive and closed the back door.

She walked over to Isabel and put her arms around her. 'I'll never forget you,' she said softly. 'Thank you for being a friend and—I have to go. I can't explain but don't blame Damien.'

Isabel hugged her then took out her hanky.

But a parting just as hard was still to come.

Tottie was sitting disconsolately beside the open driver's door.

'Oh,' Harriet said softly as a knot of emotion she'd been hoping to keep under a tight rein unravelled and her tears started to fall. 'I don't know what to say, Tottie, but I will miss you so much.' She knelt down and put her arms around the big dog. 'I'm sorry but I have to go.'

* * *

A few minutes later she was driving down the long, winding drive.

In her rear-view mirror she watched Isabel hold on to Tottie's collar so she couldn't chase after Harriet, then the house was out of sight and the double gateposts were approaching and the tears she'd held on to so tightly started to fall.

There was a sign on the road to be aware of a concealed driveway entrance to Heathcote.

There was no sign inside Heathcote to the effect that the portion of the road that went past the gates was hidden from view due to some big trees and a slight bend in it.

Still, Harriet had negotiated this many times so perhaps it was because that she was crying and had misted up her glasses that accounted for the fact that an ambulance driving into the property took her completely by surprise and caused her to swing the wheel and drive into one of the gateposts.

* * *

Damien put Harriet carefully into a chair and said in a weary, totally exasperated way, 'What the hell am I going to do with you?'

'Nothing,' Harriet responded tautly and eyed him with considerable annoyance.

They were in the flat above the studio, where all Harriet's belongings had been unloaded from Brett's vehicle and where she now sat in an armchair with one foot swathed in bandages and resting on a footstool.

The ambulance had picked Charlie and Damien up from Ballina airport because, due to his casts and stitches, fitting into a normal vehicle would have been difficult for Charlie.

The ambulance had escaped unscathed from the incident at the gate. So, yet again, had Brett's four-wheel drive. The gatepost was another matter. It had collapsed into a pile of rubble. And Harriet had somehow sprained her ankle.

The male nurse accompanying Charlie had attended to it.

'Nothing,' Harriet repeated, 'and I would appreciate it if you didn't tower over me like that or treat me like an idiot!'

'My apologies,' Damien said dryly and sat down opposite her. 'It's not the first time this has happened, however.'

'And it might not have happened if…if people hadn't made…hadn't cast aspersions on my driving or if I hadn't been…' She shook her head and closed her eyes. 'It doesn't matter.'

'Been crying?' he suggested.

Her lashes lifted. 'How did you know that?'

He grimaced. 'You looked as if you'd been crying— red eyes, you still had tears in your eyes, as a matter of fact, and tearstains on your cheeks.'

There was a longish pause, then she said, 'It was only Tottie I was crying over.' She paused. 'And perhaps Isabel.'

'Despite her aspersions on your driving?'

'How did you know *that*?'

'She told me. She feels very guilty and has asked me to apologise.'

Harriet shrugged. 'She meant well,' she said gruffly.

'So there's no possibility there was a skerrick of regret in you about leaving me?'

An uneasy silence developed until Harriet said carefully, 'You know it could never have worked, Damien.'

'I know I made a tactical error in asking you to marry me there and then. My intentions were the best, though.'

'Yes.' Harriet looked across at him. 'You thought I'd go into a decline if you didn't. You thought it could all be worked out on a pragmatic basis. Above all, you had me on your conscience again.'

'Maybe,' he said. 'But look, we're both stuck here for a while so we need to come to an arrangement.'

Harriet raised an eyebrow. 'You're staying?'

He nodded. 'I've postponed Africa while Charlie recovers.'

'I should be fine within a week at the most. It's only a sprain.'

'It's quite a severe sprain. The nurse told you to take it easy for at least a fortnight.'

'I could go crazy in a fortnight,' Harriet said gloomily.

'Not if you start on the paintings.'

She turned her head to look out of the window at the scudding clouds. 'Back to the paintings again. They're starting to haunt me.'

'Of course we could spend a few days in Hawaii or Tahiti.' His glance was ironic. 'Together,' he added and favoured her with a loaded glance.

Harriet took a sharp breath but what she was about to say went unuttered as Tottie was at last allowed into the flat, with Isabel close behind.

And Damien Wyatt observed the reunion between his aunt, his dog and—the thorn in his side?—not a bad description, he decided, and found himself feeling so annoyed on all fronts, he took himself off to, as he told them, go and see how Charlie was.

But Charlie still had the nurse with him, checking him out.

So Damien continued on to his study, but that wasn't a good idea either. That brought back memories of a girl who'd loved him in a way that could only be described as 'all or nothing'.

It also reminded him that he still fancied Harriet Livingstone, although he was undoubtedly angry with her. Angry with her for turning him down again? Angry with her for driving into the gatepost?

'Just plain angry with her,' he mused and, coming to a sudden decision, reached for the phone as he swung his feet up onto the desk.

Fortunately Arthur answered. Exchanging inanities with Penny would have been too much for him, Damien decided.

'Arthur,' he said, 'Damien. Can you spare a bit of time up here at Heathcote?'

Arthur rubbed the bridge of his nose. 'Well,

Penny is pregnant so I don't like to leave her, not for too long anyway.'

'How pregnant *is* Penny?'

'About five months.'

For crying out loud, Arthur, Damien thought but did not say, she's going to keep you dancing attendance for the next four months!

He cleared his throat. 'Uh…of course. It's just that Harriet could do with some help.'

'Harriet?' Arthur repeated. 'I thought she was fine and almost finished.'

'She was. She is finished but I've suggested she cleans the paintings for us rather than sending them away.'

'Wonderful idea,' Arthur responded heartily. 'I'm sure she'd do a great job!'

'Yes, well, she doesn't quite see it that way and that's probably because she's a bit incapacitated at the moment. But I thought if you could come up and go through them with her—you know, if she had someone to discuss them with, someone who really knows what they're talking about, it could help.'

There was a short silence then Arthur said on a curious note, 'Incapacitated?'

'She's sprained her ankle.'

'How?'

Damien grimaced. 'She…ran into the gate-post. In that…tank.'

A sudden silence came down the line, then, 'I don't believe it! The girl's a menace behind the wheel.'

'Uh, there may have been extenuating circum-stances.'

'What?' Arthur enquired. 'A dog or two that escaped completely unscathed?'

Damien's lips twisted. 'No. But anyway, she's a bit down in the dumps and I didn't—' he paused and was struck by a brainwave '—I didn't be-lieve Penny would like to think of Harriet like that.'

'Of course not,' Arthur agreed. 'I'll come up tomorrow morning. How's Charlie?'

* * *

Damien put the phone down a few minutes later. Then he lifted the receiver again and proceeded to order not one but two wheelchairs, and two pairs of crutches.

CHAPTER NINE

'How's Penny?'

Harriet and Arthur were in the dining room and Arthur was pushing her around in a wheelchair from painting to painting. Harriet was taking notes.

'Well, we were expecting morning sickness, of course, and *some* form of—I don't know—maybe emotional highs and lows, some weird cravings like pickles on jam, but she doesn't seem to have *ever* been better.'

Harriet hid a smile. Arthur sounded quite worried.

'That's *good* news,' she said. 'Sounds as if she's having an uncomplicated pregnancy. Oh!' Harriet stared at a picture on the wall. 'I can't believe I never noticed that before.'

'Tom Roberts. Heidelberg School. One of my favourites. I was lucky to get that,' Arthur said complacently

'I love his beach scenes,' Harriet said dreamily. 'Where did you find it?'

Arthur pushed her a bit further on and into the hall as he told her the story of how he'd acquired the Tom Roberts for Damien's father. Harriet listened, genuinely fascinated, and they spent a pleasurable couple of hours going through the Wyatt collection.

In fact, when they'd finished and he'd wheeled her back to the studio, Harriet said energetically, 'Arthur, I'll need—'

'I'll get all the stuff you need, Harriet. It's quite some time since they were last done—I've been urging Damien to do it for a while so I'm really pleased he's asked you. You seem to—' he eyed Tottie, who was lying next to the wheelchair '—fit in here really well, too.'

Harriet opened her mouth to dispute this but

that could only sound churlish, so she simply nodded.

He went shortly thereafter but sought Damien out before driving off.

He was up in his study, which gave Arthur a sense of déjà vu.

'Come in,' Damien responded to his triple knock.

'Mission accomplished,' Arthur said. 'She's going to do them. She even sounds quite enthusiastic about it now.'

'Thanks, mate.'

Arthur fingered his blue waistcoat with purple airships on it as he pulled up a chair. 'Unusual girl that, you know.'

Damien couldn't help a swift glance at the settee across the room, and made the sudden unspoken decision to have it moved elsewhere. 'Yes, I do, as a matter of fact,' he replied dryly.

'Penny reckons it's a case of still waters running deep with Harriet Livingstone and she doubts she'll ever get over Simon Dexter.'

Damien frowned. 'I thought they hadn't seen each other since college when they bumped into each other, Penny and Harriet?'

'They hadn't, but word gets around and Penny has quite a network of old friends, so when Harriet bobbed up—she did some research, you might say. And—'

'Simon *Dexter*,' Damien interrupted. 'Elite golfer who's earned himself a million dollars recently, playboy, heart-throb—that Simon Dexter?'

Arthur nodded. 'Can't imagine what brought them together in the first place. I mean, she's not a groupie type, she's not a sporting type. The way she keeps running into things suggests she may even be a bit uncoordinated, not to mention short-sighted.'

'Suffers from a left-handed syndrome, in fact,' Damien supplied.

'Never heard of it.'

'That makes two of us. Uh…hasn't Simon

Dexter been on the news lately—for other reasons?'

'Could well have been; I haven't been much tuned into the news lately. And I should be getting home.' Arthur stood up. 'You'll have your hands full, what with Charlie and Harriet, but at least her—er—incarceration, if you could call it that, is only for a couple of weeks.'

'Yes.'

And, to Arthur's surprise, after that single yes, Damien seemed to fall into some kind of reverie and didn't appear to notice his departure.

By the time Arthur had gone, Harriet was also deep in thought for a time.

Along the lines of wondering whether she'd been conned into staying on and doing the paintings.

Surely not. She could hardly be in Damien Wyatt's good books at the moment, after knocking back both his proposals as well as knocking down his gatepost.

But he had rung Arthur and Arthur had tapped

into her love of art and managed to imbue her with a feeling of enthusiasm, even eagerness for the project.

Why, though? Why would he want her to stay on?

She shook her head and her thoughts returned to Arthur and how, despite his waistcoats, she enjoyed talking to him about art.

Arthur, she thought with a fond little smile. How on earth was he going to get through the rest of Penny's pregnancy, let alone the birth?

The next morning her ankle was more swollen than it had been, and more painful, so Charlie's nurse conceded that there might be something broken and she should have an X-ray. Isabel drove her in to Lismore, where an X-ray revealed a hairline fracture and a cast was applied to her ankle. She was warned to keep her weight off it while it healed.

Easier said than done, as she discovered. She

was exhausted after hopping up the stairs to the flat on one foot, even with Isabel's help.

'We'll have to do something about this,' Isabel said worriedly. 'You can't go through this every time you want to get out or home. Damien should have thought of that. I'll speak to him.'

'Don't worry about it,' Harriet told her. 'Just please say hello to Charlie. And tell him in a few days I'll actually get to see him.'

Isabel went away, still looking worried.

And, an hour or so later, Isabel, Stan and Damien mounted the steps to the flat and moved Harriet and her belongings down to the ground floor of the house.

She didn't protest. She didn't have the energy.

Her new quarters were a guest suite, with a sitting room and separate bedroom, pretty and floral and comfortable, with a view over the garden.

Isabel unpacked for her and brought her a cup of tea but she was alone when Damien came in with a knock and closed the door behind him. He didn't beat about the bush.

'What's wrong?'

Harriet stared up at him, and licked her lips. 'What do you mean?' she asked huskily. 'I...I've broken a bone in my ankle.'

He sat down opposite her wheelchair. 'I know that but I was wondering—' he paused '—whether you'd heard that Simon Dexter and his wife Carol have split up.'

Harriet gasped and her eyes widened.

'It's been on the news. He's a newsworthy figure nowadays. More so perhaps than when you knew him?'

'Yes.' She stared at him. 'I...I...no, I hadn't heard.'

'Do you play golf?' he asked.

'Oh, no!'

'I thought you might have had golf lessons in similar circumstances to your riding lessons.'

'No.' She shook her head.

'So how did you and Simon Dexter get together?'

Harriet looked away and clasped her hands in her lap.

'Don't tell me,' Damien said softly as a tide of pink entered her cheeks, 'that you ran into him?'

She said stiffly, 'Not with a car. Well, not exactly a car.'

'I hesitate to wonder what "not exactly a car" could be,' he marvelled.

Harriet tossed him an irate look. 'A golf buggy, of course.'

'Of course! How dumb can I get? How did it happen?'

'My father did play golf. I was going around with him one morning when he asked me to drive the buggy up to the green while he made a shot from the rough and then took a shortcut not suitable for buggies, to the green. I'd never driven one before but it seemed pretty simple.' She raised her eyebrows. 'Famous last thoughts.'

'You obviously didn't kill Simon or maim him.'

'No.' Harriet paused and a frown grew in her

eyes. 'How did you know it was Simon Dexter? I didn't think I mentioned his surname.'

Damien studied his hands for a moment then grimaced. 'Arthur.'

'Arthur doesn't know him.'

'Penny, then.'

'Penny doesn't know him either,' Harriet objected.

'Ah, but Penny runs this spy ring, MI55. She's actually M in disguise, or—' he raised an eyebrow '—is she Miss Moneypenny?'

Harriet went from bristling to calming down to smiling involuntarily. 'I still don't understand how it came up,' she said, though.

'We were worried that you seemed to be down in the dumps.'

She took a breath and sat back. 'I don't know how I feel. I—it's terribly sad actually, isn't it?'

He didn't agree or disagree. He posed a question instead. 'So what is it?'

'What is what?'

'If it's not Simon Dexter, what's making you look as if your heart's breaking?'

Harriet swallowed. 'I didn't know I was. Look, it's probably just my ankle, bound up with feeling like a fool and…' She tailed off.

He raised his eyebrows. 'In what way?'

Harriet sighed. 'Surely I don't have to spell it out for you?'

He rubbed his jaw. 'You're regretting knocking back my offers of marriage?' Sheer irony glinted in his dark eyes.

'I'd be a fool to want to be married to you after…after what happened with your first wife—and how it affected you,' she said slowly. 'No. I feel stupid, that's all.'

Damien studied her thoughtfully. Her hair was clipped back to within an inch of its life—no wavy tendrils today, as there'd been on the night of Charlie's birthday party, no discreet make-up to emphasise her stunning eyes, no shimmering lipstick rendering those severe lips doubly inviting.

No gorgeous dress that showed off those amazing legs—not only tracksuit trousers today but a cast on her ankle… So what was it about her that made how she looked a matter of indifference to him?

It struck him suddenly that she was the most unaware girl he'd ever known. She certainly didn't flash her legs. She didn't bat those long eyelashes except when she was thinking seriously and tended to blink.

Was that why it didn't matter whether she was dressed up or down—he still fancied her? Then he was struck by a thought.

'You're not,' he said at last, with his eyes suddenly widening, 'pregnant, are you?'

Harriet opened and closed her mouth. 'No.'

'I'm sorry,' he said dryly. 'That wasn't a very good way of phrasing things, but if you are—'

'I'm not,' she broke in.

'Sure?'

Harriet eyed him. 'Yes.'

They stared at each other for a long moment,

she with a spark of anger in her eyes, he suddenly completely inscrutable.

'Harriet,' he said, 'there's no point in hiding it from me.'

'I'm not hiding anything from you!' she protested. 'It was—unlikely, anyway.'

'That has been a trap for the unwary since time immemorial,' he said dryly. 'We both stand convicted of thoughtlessness there, however.' He shrugged and a glint of humour lit his eyes. 'Could we blame Charlie?'

'Blame Charlie for what? Thanks, mate,' Charlie said to his male nurse as he was pushed into the guest suite. 'Harriet! I can't believe we're both in wheelchairs!'

'Charlie!' Harriet had to laugh because, from the neck up, it was the same old Charlie and his infectious smile and mischievous expression hadn't changed. Otherwise, he had his right arm in a cast and a sling and his left leg stretched out in a cast.

'Oh, Charlie!' She hoisted herself out of her

wheelchair and hopped across to him on one foot to kiss him warmly. 'I'm so glad to see you, even if you did render us thoughtless! Oh, nothing,' she said to Charlie's puzzled look. 'Nothing!'

They had dinner together that night.

The new cook produced barbecued swordfish on skewers with a salad, followed by a brandy pudding.

'Mmm,' Charlie said, 'if he doesn't burn down the kitchen, he may be as good as old cookie.'

'She,' Isabel contributed. 'I decided there'd be less chance of that with a woman.'

I can't believe I'm doing this, Harriet thought. I can't believe I'm sitting here like one of the family after actually driving away from Heathcote and planning to stay away for ever. I can't believe Damien is doing the same!

She glanced across at him but found his expression difficult to read, except to think that he looked withdrawn.

* * *

After dinner, however, everyone seemed to go their separate ways.

Charlie's nurse insisted he go to bed. Isabel went out to a meeting after wheeling Harriet into the guest suite and Damien went up to his study.

Harriet sat for several minutes in the wheelchair then decided she was exhausted. She used the crutches Damien had hired to get herself changed and finally into bed.

She was sitting up in bed arranging a pillow under her foot when she remembered she hadn't locked the door and she was just about to remedy this when the outer door clicked opened and Damien walked in.

Harriet went to say something but her voice refused to work and she had to clear her throat.

He must have heard because, with a light tap on the open door, he came through to the bedroom.

'OK?' He stood at the end of the bed and studied her in her ruffled grey nightgown.

Harriet nodded. 'Fine, thanks. Have you come to…?' Her eyes were wide and questioning.

'I haven't come to take up residence,' he said rather dryly. 'I've come to talk.'

'Oh.'

His lips twisted. 'What would you have said if I'd indicated otherwise?'

Harriet swallowed. 'I'm not sure.'

He studied her comprehensively then turned away and pulled a chair up. 'If you're worried about staying on to do the paintings, can I make a couple of points?' He didn't wait for her approval. 'You really seem to enjoy this place, you love art and I guess—' he grimaced '—it's not a bad place to convalesce.' He paused and listened for a moment, then grinned and got up to let Tottie in.

She came up to the bed and rested her muzzle next to Harriet.

Harriet's eyes softened as she stroked the dog's nose. 'I've left you once, with disastrous consequences,' she murmured. 'Could I do it again?'

'You don't have to,' Damien said. 'There's something else you could do. I told you Charlie plays chess?'

She nodded after a moment.

'He's going to need some help to get through this period. Obviously he can't spend the whole time playing chess, but you two might be able to come up with ways to keep each other occupied—you're going to have the same problem for a while. You can't spend your life cleaning paintings.'

Harriet looked up at him. 'What about you?'

'What about me?'

She sat up and plaited her fingers. 'Will you be here?'

'Yes. But I'll be busy. Africa is coming to me, you see.'

Harriet blinked several times. 'Come again?'

He grimaced. 'I've reversed things. Instead of taking my machinery there, I've invited this company I'm dealing with to come here. I may not—' he paused then continued gravely '—be able to offer them wildlife safaris with lions, leopards, buffalo, elephants and hippos, to name a few, but there's the Great Barrier Reef, the Kimberley, Cape York, Arnheim Land and some wonderful fishing. If they feel like a bit of danger there are plenty of crocodiles to dodge.'

Harriet blinked again then had to laugh. 'Is that what big business is all about?'

'That's better... It has a part.'

'What's better?' Harriet asked curiously.

He shrugged after a moment. 'It's the first time I've seen you laugh since you demolished the gatepost.

'But look, I'll obviously be here at times. If you're worried I'm liable to harass you on the subject of...on any subject, don't be.'

Harriet turned her attention to Tottie, still sitting patiently beside the bed, and wondered at the reaction his statement brought to her. It had a familiar feeling to it...

But Damien didn't elaborate. He felt in his pocket for his phone, and glanced at the screen.

'Sorry,' he murmured. 'I need to take this. Sleep well.' And he walked out, switching off the over-head lights so that she only had her bedside lamp to deal with. Tottie pattered after him at a click of his fingers. He closed the door.

She lay back after a moment and turned the bedside lamp off. And she pulled the spare pil-low into her arms and hugged it as she exam-ined that familiar feeling she'd experienced only minutes ago on hearing he didn't intend to ha-rass her.

Why should that make her feel hollow and lonely at the same time as she felt ruffled and restless? It didn't make sense. She should be re-lieved if anything. The last thing she should feel like was crying herself to sleep.

It could never work—any other arrangement with Damien could never work; she knew that in her heart and soul, didn't she? It would hurt her dreadfully if she came to be mistrusted be-cause he couldn't help it now; if she could never get right though to him, if she lost him…

But how to cope with *this* hurt. Living in the same house with him, even if he wasn't home a lot, wanting him, wanting to be special to him, loving him...

CHAPTER TEN

THREE MONTHS LATER there were no more wheel-chairs or crutches at Heathcote.

Both Charlie and Harriet were recovered, Harriet completely, Charlie almost there; and Damien Wyatt had been as good as his word. Then again, he'd hardly spent any time at Heathcote at all.

But he came home one evening, three months on, with the news that he'd swung his South African deal at last, which was exceedingly good news, he told them, but he needed a break.

'So I'll be home for a while,' he said, laying his napkin down on the table. He still wore a grey suit with a blue shirt but he'd discarded his tie. 'By the way, that dessert was almost up to your standards, Harriet,' he added.

'It was up to her standard—it was hers,' Isabel said.

Damien looked down the table at Harriet. 'How come?'

'Uh...' Harriet hesitated.

'The new cook proved to have light fingers in more ways than one,' Charlie said. 'She was a good cook, made marvellous pastry, actually, but when we began to discover we were missing minor amounts of money—you know what it's like, at first you think maybe you were mistaken and you didn't have it or you'd spent it or whatever, but then not only did it happen more often but she got bolder and took larger amounts.'

'So you fired her,' Damien said to Isabel.

'I didn't exactly fire her; she has an elderly mother to support. I...I let her go. I haven't found anyone to replace her yet, so Harriet very kindly stepped into her shoes.'

'What would we do without Harriet?' Damien murmured. 'But what is it about Heathcote that attracts either arsonists or petty thieves?'

'Cookie wasn't really an arsonist,' Isabel argued. 'Just…careless.'

Damien grimaced then pushed back his chair. 'OK, well, thanks, Harriet. And could you spare me a few moments of your time? I'll be upstairs in my study.'

Isabel said she would deal with the dishes and Harriet closed herself into the flat above the studio. She'd insisted on moving out of the house once she was mobile again.

Her emotions now, three months on and having received what had almost amounted to an order to beard Damien in his den, were hard to define.

He'd almost made it sound, she marvelled with clenched fists, as if she'd gone out of her way to make herself indispensable to the Wyatt family; as if she had a secret agenda to her own advantage.

When, if she was honest, the last three months *had* had a secret agenda, they'd been mostly sheer torture for her.

When he'd been home she'd had to use all her willpower to be normal and unaffected in his presence. When he'd been gone, it had taken all her willpower not to pack her bags and run for cover. But that would have meant deserting not only Brett but Charlie.

The other sticking point had been the Heathcote paintings. Her estimation of a month to clean them had proved to be optimistic. Even if she'd worked as tirelessly as she had for the most part over his mother's treasures, she'd have taken longer than a month.

But trying to keep Charlie occupied at the same time—until she'd had a brainwave—had slowed her down a lot. The brainwave had been to introduce Charlie to Brett. They'd hit it off immediately.

Her other sticking point with the paintings had been the generous amount she'd already been paid—Damien had simply paid the money into her account without consulting her.

The result was she felt honour-bound to either

finish the job or pay the money back. But Brett still had some treatment to go through…

All this, though, she reasoned as she pulled on a blue cardigan over her shirt and jeans, was minor compared to the other inner havoc she'd experienced. The lonely nights when he was only a few steps away from her—that knowledge had kept her tossing and turning.

The lonely nights when she had no idea where he was—or who he was with.

The frisson that ran though her every time she walked through the dining room and recalled their first meeting and that passionate embrace. Recalled the feel of him, the taste of him, his wandering touch that had lit a fuse of sensation within her—if he had a problem with the lounge, her nemesis was the dining room, the memory had never gone away…

And now this, she thought.

A hard, bright, difficult Damien who'd ordered her up to his study as if she were a schoolgirl. A room she hadn't been in since the night

Charlie…don't even think about it, she warned herself.

Despite the stern warning to herself, she stood outside the study for a couple of moments, trying to compose herself. Then she knocked and went in. Tottie followed her.

He was lounging behind his desk. There was a silver tray with a coffee pot and two cups on the desk. The windows were open on an unusually warm spring night and there was the sound and the salty air of the sea wafting in.

'Ah,' Damien said. 'I see you've brought your reinforcement.'

Harriet pushed her hair behind her ears. 'If you don't want her here—'

'Of course I don't mind her being here,' he said irritably. 'She *is* my dog. Sit down.'

Harriet looked around and froze. There was no longer the settee where they had… She stopped that thought in its tracks. Instead there were two elegant chairs covered in navy leather.

'You… I…' She turned back to Damien. 'I

mean…nothing.' She swallowed and pulled one of the chairs up but was unable to stop herself from blushing a bright pink as she sat down. Tottie arranged herself at her feet.

Damien steepled his fingers beneath his chin and studied her meditatively. 'You think I should have kept it, the settee? As a memorial of some kind?'

Harriet's blush deepened but she said, 'No. I mean—' she gestured '—it was entirely up to you. What did you want to see me about?'

He stared at her then said abruptly, 'What are we going to do?'

'Do?' Harriet blinked.

'I hesitate to remind you, Harriet Livingstone, but that's exactly what you said to me once before in highly similar circumstances. The day we first met here.'

Her eyes widened.

'I asked you what we were going to do and you repeated "do" as if—as if nothing had ever happened between us or, if it had, it meant nothing,' he said savagely.

'Y-you—' her voice quivered and, to her amazement, she heard herself go on '—got rid of the settee. As if it meant nothing.'

'I didn't get rid of it,' he denied. 'I had it moved to my bedroom, just in case I should be plagued by any erotic images of you during a business meeting.'

Harriet blinked and this time her cheeks grew so hot she had to put her hands up to cover them. 'I can't believe I…said that.'

He looked darkly amused for a moment. 'Maybe your innermost sentiments got the upper hand. Harriet, we can't go on like this. I can't anyway.'

He sat back and Harriet was suddenly shocked to see how tired he looked.

She opened her mouth but he waved a hand to forestall her. 'Don't say it. I know what you'll say anyway. You'll offer to go, just like you did the last time. Well, it's been a couple of times now but I can't guarantee a gatepost for you to drive into this time.'

'Wh…what do you suggest?' she asked. 'You say we can't go on like this but you don't want me to go.'

'Marry me,' he said after a long tense pause. 'I've given you three months to recover from Simon Dexter and your best friend Carol.'

Harriet gasped. 'You didn't have to—' She stopped abruptly. 'I mean…I mean there's still Veronica, there's still the way you feel—'

His dark eyes were mocking. 'You have no idea how I feel. I had no idea what it was all about so there was no way you could have known,' he said.

'I don't understand.' Harriet blinked almost frenziedly.

'Then I'll tell you.' He sat forward. 'I can't cope any more.'

'I still don't understand.'

'Harriet—' he fiddled with a pen for a long

moment then looked into her eyes '—can I tell you a story?'

She nodded.

'I couldn't…right from the beginning I couldn't get you out of my mind. I told you that was why I agreed to see you again?'

'Two months later, though. I mean—I don't mean to nit-pick but it was that.'

He grimaced. 'You're entitled to nit-pick. But from then on I couldn't get you out of my mind. I couldn't believe you were still driving that ghastly old tank and I had to do something about it. I couldn't believe how much I worried about you. I couldn't believe how I kept coming up with jobs for you. I couldn't believe,' he said dryly, 'how the thought of your legs kept interfering with my sex life.'

Her lips parted. 'You mean…?' She looked incredulous.

'It's true. After I kissed you the first time,' he said wryly, 'I decided I'd either gone a bit mad or I needed some nice girl who understood the rules—no wedding bells, in other words—and I found a couple. But the trouble was, they had ordinary legs.'

Harriet put a hand to her mouth. 'I don't believe this,' she said indistinctly.

'You should,' he replied. 'Of course, it wasn't only their legs. I simply didn't seem to be attracted to anyone any more—anyone who wasn't you, that is.'

'Are you serious?'

He studied her wide eyes and the look of shock in them. 'I've never been more serious, I've never been as confused, as I was for a while, in my whole life. I've never felt as rejected as I did the night of Charlie's accident when you…'

'Don't.' Harriet closed her eyes briefly. 'I felt terrible then, and the night of his birthday party.'

'Good,' he said gravely but his eyes were wicked.

She bit her lip. 'I did seriously not want to be on your conscience, though, I still do,' she said then with more spirit. 'I mean I still don't want to be—there,' she elucidated.

'I know what you mean and you're not. It's something else altogether and it only started to come home to me when you ran into the gate-post.'

'Don't,' she pleaded. 'Don't bring up those things. They meant nothing.'

'Maybe not to you but they did to me. They were all part of the picture, you see.'

'What picture?' She frowned at him.

'The picture I loved. I *loved* you, Harriet Livingstone. That's why I cared so much about you. The thing I'd thought could *never* happen for me, had snuck up and hit me on the head, and I realised I was going to spend the rest of my *life* worrying about you.'

They gazed at each other and she thought he suddenly looked pale.

'And loving you because I just can't help my-self. All the rest of it, all my grudges and heaven knows what else, they suddenly counted for nothing.'

'Damien,' she whispered.

'Nothing had the power to change that or flaw it or make the slightest difference to how I felt about you. Remember the night you told me you weren't pregnant?'

She nodded.

'I couldn't believe how disappointed I was.'

Harriet stared at him with her lips parted. 'But…but you went away. You told me you wouldn't be harassing me on—on any subject.'

He grimaced. 'And I even managed to stick to that. But don't forget you told me that same day that you'd be a fool to want to be married to me after Veronica and how it had left me. You also hadn't had time to absorb the news about Simon Dexter and your best friend. And I thought—' He stopped abruptly.

'What?' she asked.

'That I could never get you to believe me.' He looked suddenly irritated to death. 'Especially after I'd told you *why* it was no good us contemplating any future together.' He gestured. 'I was also afraid that you could never love me.'

'Never love you?'

He froze as she repeated the phrase as if it had never occurred to her.

'Harriet,' he said ominously, 'you told me at the beginning that you were quite happy to remain fancy-free and you never, even after you slept with me, changed your position other than to a slight tinge of regret when I told you about Veronica!'

'Damien,' she said, 'can I tell you my story? It's not as long as yours but that slight tinge of regret you sensed when you told me about Veronica was in fact a torrent of sudden understanding. I *was* determined to stay "fancy free", I'd fooled myself into thinking I had but it suddenly hit me—that I'd fallen head over heels in love with you and it was the saddest moment of my life.'

He got up and came cautiously round the desk,

almost as if he was feeling his way in the dark. 'You said you were sad about Simon.'

'No.' She shook her head. 'I was sad for Carol.' She shrugged.

'So.' He sat down on the corner of the desk. 'Have I been living in hell for these long months because I was a blind fool?' He pulled her upright and into his arms.

'I wouldn't say that. I guess we both had our demons.' She put her hands on his upper arms and all restraint suddenly vanished as they were consumed by an overwhelming hunger.

Harriet felt the blood surging through her veins as if she were on fire at his lightest touch. She felt incredibly aware of her body and of his. But it was more than that for Harriet, more than a sensual arousal that rocked them both; it was a feeling of safety, as if she'd come home, as if a part of her that had been wrenched away had been restored to her.

And when they drew apart she was crying as well as laughing, she was in a state of shock that told Damien more than words could how deep her feelings were.

'Harriet. Harriet,' he said into her hair as he cradled her in his arms, 'it's OK. We've made it. Don't cry.'

'I can't help it. I'm so happy.'

'Come.' He picked her up.

'Where?' she queried.

'You'll see.'

He took her to his bedroom, not the one his parents had used, not the one he'd shared with Veronica—a different room but with a familiar settee along one wall.

'See?' He put her down on it and sat down beside her.

Her tears changed to laughter. 'I couldn't believe how that upset me, the thought that you'd got rid of it!'

His lips twisted. 'You've no idea how good that is to hear.'

'Why?' she queried innocently

'Well, this old settee has brought back some memories.' He allowed his dark gaze to roam over her figure.

'I thought it might be something like that.' Her eyes glinted with humour but only for a moment, then desire replaced the humour and she put her hands on his shoulders, and hesitated.

He frowned. 'What is it?'

'Some other memories. The first time you kissed me it crossed my mind that you knew how to make love to a woman in a way that thrilled her and drove her to excesses she didn't know she could reach... I was right. That night and this settee proved it to me. It had never happened to me like that before. I didn't—' she smiled wryly '—quite recognise myself, even if I had believed I was an all or nothing person.'

Damien stared into her eyes for a long, long moment.

'Harriet,' he said finally, in a husky voice un-like his own, 'if you continue to make incendiary statements like that—we may never get off this settee.'

She laughed then they sobered and their need for each other was so great it wasn't only the settee that became involved but the floor then the bed.

'So you will marry me?' he said when they were lying in each other's arms, sated and in the dreamy aftermath of their passion.

'Yes.' She ran her fingers through his hair.

'Tomorrow?'

Harriet laughed softly. 'I don't think you can do it that fast but if you could I would.'

'On the other hand, coming back to reality, if we're going to do this,' he reflected, 'we might as well do it with style. Not big but with style.'

'Do you think I look all right?' Harriet said to Isabel two weeks later.

She was dressed and ready for her wedding.

She wore a white dress with lacy sleeves and a bouffant skirt that skimmed her knees. Her hair was fair, glossy and coaxed into ringlets. But she stared at herself in the bedroom mirror and sighed.

'You look beautiful,' Isabel replied. She'd been in a state of constant excitement ever since the wedding had been announced.

Harriet sighed again, however, as she continued to gaze at her reflection in the mirror.

'What?' Isabel queried as she produced a pair of new shoes out of a box for Harriet.

'It's just that when I first met Damien I looked a mess. Then, the next time we met, I looked like an attendant out of a museum. I'm just wondering if he doesn't prefer me looking—unusual.' She sat down on the bed to put her new shoes on.

'Honey,' Isabel said, 'believe me, he will love this you as much as all the others.'

'*You* look lovely,' Harriet said, taking in Isabel's camellia-pink linen suit. 'And I can't thank you enough for…for everything. You've been marvellous.'

Isabel sat down on the bed next to Harriet and

picked up her hand. 'I knew someone once,' she said. 'I thought he was my north and my south but I wasn't prepared to play second fiddle to his career. And it would have meant a lot of time on my own. It would have meant bringing up our kids virtually on my own, it would have meant being the other woman to a career that was almost like a mistress to him. So I said no when he mentioned marriage.'

Isabel paused and looked into the distance. 'I sent him away and I've regretted it ever since.'

Harriet caught her breath. 'Can't—surely you could have—wasn't there some way you could have got together again?'

Isabel shook her head. 'By the time I'd realised what I'd done, and it took a few years to *really* realise it, he'd married someone else. So—' Isabel patted Harriet's hand again '—to see you and Damien so much in love and getting married when I was afraid it wasn't going to happen, when I thought it all was going to fail, means a lot to me.'

'Now you've made me cry!'

'Here, just fix your make-up and you'll be fine. But first, let me do this.' And she hugged Harriet warmly.

It was a beautiful day and the garden was looking its finest.

There was a table set up for the marriage celebrant with a cloth of gold and a marvellous bouquet of flowers fresh picked from the garden that morning. There were chairs set out for the guests on the lawn and there was a sumptuous buffet laid out on the veranda.

The guests, more than Harriet had expected, comprised close family friends and, of course, family. Charlie was there—apart from the slightest limp, he was quite recovered from his accident and he'd brought along a stunning brunette. He was also the best man.

Brett Livingstone was there, also almost fully mobile now and engaged to his physiotherapist. It was he who was to give Harriet away.

Arthur and Penny Tindall were there. Arthur wore a morning suit.

Harriet drew a very deep breath as she stepped out from her guest suite and paused for a moment.

Brett was waiting for her. And Damien who, thanks to Isabel's sense of tradition, she had not seen since yesterday, was waiting at the table in the garden with Charlie by his side.

'Ready?' Brett mouthed, his eyes full of affection as he held out his arm.

She nodded and something brushed against her legs—Tottie. Tottie, with a ribbon in her collar and a wide smile, as if to say, *It's OK. I'm here.*

Then she was beside Damien, who was looking quite breathtakingly handsome in a dark suit. And Brett stepped back, leaving her to her fate...

They exchanged a long glance that sent tremors through Harriet because that was the effect Damien had on her and always would, she suspected. Then his lips twisted and a wicked little glint lit his eyes. 'I like your dress. I was afraid you'd wear something long.'

'I was afraid you mightn't marry me if I did,' she whispered back.

'For crying out loud, who mightn't marry whom? Don't tell me you two are having second thoughts!' Charlie intervened, although sotto voce. 'I'm a nervous wreck already.'

'Why?' Damien and Harriet asked simultaneously.

'In case I lost the ring or dropped it or did something otherwise stupid.' He ran his finger round his neck inside his collar. 'Damn nerve-racking business this getting married bit. I might have second thoughts about it myself!'

Both Harriet and Damien laughed and the marriage celebrant cleared her throat and asked if she could proceed.

All three participants in front of her replied in the affirmative in a rather heartfelt manner, so she did.

Not many minutes later, Damien Richard

Wyatt and Harriet Margaret Livingstone were pronounced man and wife and the bridegroom was told he might kiss the bride.

Damien put his arms around her. 'I *love* you,' he said and bent his head to kiss her lips.

But, at that moment, Penny Tindall, who had a rather penetrating voice, said, 'Arthur…Arthur, the baby's coming!'

And before the bemused gaze of the whole congregation plus the bridal party, Arthur Tindall sprang to his feet, and fainted.

'Things are running true to form,' Damien said to Harriet. 'There's something about us getting within a cooee of each other that just invites chaos!'

They laughed together and went to rescue Arthur.

'It was always my deepest fear,' Arthur said that evening as he clutched a glass of brandy, 'that I would have to deliver the baby. That's what did it. That's what made me faint.'

In fact Penny's baby had been delivered in a maternity ward, as planned, admittedly after a rather fast trip in an ambulance, but both mother and daughter were fine.

* * * * *

Mills & Boon® Large Print
July 2014

0614 Rom LP

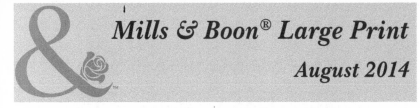

Mills & Boon® Large Print
August 2014

A D'ANGELO LIKE NO OTHER
Carole Mortimer

SEDUCED BY THE SULTAN
Sharon Kendrick

WHEN CHRISTAKOS MEETS HIS MATCH
Abby Green

THE PUREST OF DIAMONDS?
Susan Stephens

SECRETS OF A BOLLYWOOD MARRIAGE
Susanna Carr

WHAT THE GREEK'S MONEY CAN'T BUY
Maya Blake

THE LAST PRINCE OF DAHAAR
Tara Pammi

THE SECRET INGREDIENT
Nina Harrington

STOLEN KISS FROM A PRINCE
Teresa Carpenter

BEHIND THE FILM STAR'S SMILE
Kate Hardy

THE RETURN OF MRS JONES
Jessica Gilmore

Discover more romance at

www.millsandboon.co.uk

❤ WIN great prizes in our exclusive competitions

❤ BUY new titles before they hit the shops

❤ BROWSE new books and REVIEW your favourites

❤ SAVE on new books with the Mills & Boon® Bookclub™

❤ DISCOVER new authors

PLUS, to chat about your favourite reads, get the latest news and find special offers:

🅵 Find us on facebook.com/millsandboon

🐦 Follow us on twitter.com/millsandboonuk

❤ Sign up to our newsletter at millsandboon.co.uk